It's Only a Dream

And Other Stories

David M. Brooks

Contents

It's Only a Dream

It's Only a Dream

2016 AD

Kyle parked his jeep in the small turn-about on the side of the mountain road at the top of the hill. Reaching back, he grabbed his skateboard from the back seat, exited the jeep, and stood in the center of the road looking down the long, straight hill he had just climbed. "Stay calm," he reminded himself. "I can do this because I want to. I can do this because it's possible." Kyle bent and placed the skateboard on the blacktop, centering it on one of the white lines that dotted the middle of the road. The sky was a cloudless baby blue and the air was dry and still, a perfect summer day in northern Minnesota. The street was deserted. He had encountered no other vehicles going either direction on his short drive up the mountain side. He could hear the birds chatting back and forth in the forest that bordered the mountain road on his right and imagined them lining up in the trees to watch his daring feat. He took a long, slow breath, focused once again on the task at hand and with his left foot planted on the skateboard, his right foot pushed off from the street with three quick pumps before joining his left on the board, and he was on his way down the hill.

As he picked up speed gliding flawlessly down the center of the road, his excitement started to build and he reminded himself again to stay calm. "Breath slow and steady. I am the best mountain skateboarder on this planet. Here, now, I am God. I can do whatever I want. Stay calm."

Kyle wasn't worried about spilling off his skateboard while attaining peak speeds before reaching the tight bend in the road three quarters of a mile down the hill. He'd never seen a stray rock or a pothole or a car driving in the opposite direction. In fact, the thought that that could ever happen had never even crossed his mind. This particular hill, this precise stretch of blacktop with its sharp bend in the road after a long, straight runway, had no purpose other than that for which it now served. As far as Kyle was concerned, it had been made for this moment. The street felt as smooth as glass beneath the wheels of his skateboard and the wind started to tousle his hair. He wore no protective gear; no helmet, no knee pads or elbow pads. They just got in the way. He wore blue jean shorts and a loose-fitting, over-sized, gray Adidas t-shirt that flapped behind him with his shoulder length, brown hair in the wind as his speed increased. Holding his excitement at bay as best he could, he focused on the approaching bend.

The mountain rose to his right with tall pines and evergreens densely populating the hillside. To his left he could only see the tops of the trees over the side of the road as the mountain dropped steeply into the lush, green valley nestled below at its base. The bend in the road curved right, clinging to the side of the mountain. There was no guard rail along the left side of the bend in front of the drop, which was another reason why this particular stretch of road was perfect for Kyle.

As the bend quickened its approach, Kyle felt his adrenalin rise and tried to force himself to relax. He spied the small wooden ramp dead ahead on the edge of the road and with his arms held straight out on each side, he crouched a little lower in his stance on the board, readying his knees to act at precisely the right time.

Kyle hit the two-foot-long ramp perfectly down the center and soared out over the treetops into the open air. The skateboard fell away from his feet and into the valley a mile or so below. Kyle rose with the wind and started flying like an eagle through the valley sky between the mountains. The wind rushed against his face and smelled of fresh pine. Below him, the foothills rolled until he spotted the freeway to guide him towards town. He didn't have to flap his arms or anything silly like that to keep his speed. He just flew. Occasionally he would swoop in low and land on a high treetop for a second just to take in the view before leaping off and soaring high into the sky again until he got to town. Sometimes it took him only a minute to get there; sometimes it seemed to take an hour to fly out of the hills. He didn't mind either way. He just loved to fly.

His vision was that of a hawk. When in the air, it seemed he could zoom in visually on anything that caught his attention. He flew over his own house, circling the small lake it bordered twice and landing once on his own roof before moving on to explore other neighborhoods and towns. He was just passing over downtown Duluth when he saw the flashing red pterodactyl cross the sky below him. "Ignore it," he told himself. "Stay focused!" But it was too late. Now Kyle *was* flapping his arms like a lunatic as he began to fall out of the sky, all the while, knowing his effort to stay air born was useless. He was going down. The pterodactyl had spoken and now he had to respond.

"Damn!" Kyle muttered to himself, as he propped up on his elbow and groggily reached over the bedside table to shut off his alarm clock. He clicked on the bedside lamp, opened the single drawer of the small table, and pulled out his pen and dream log. After leafing quickly through two-thirds of the journal to find the next blank spot, he penned in the date and wrote "flying – skateboard – valley, home, downtown – two trees and a roof – fell out of sky."

Putting the pen and journal back into the drawer, he climbed out of bed and headed for the bathroom. He brushed his teeth and then checked the mirror closely to see if his prematurely receding hairline had made any progress while he had slept. He didn't think it had, but that kind of thing always seemed to sneak up on you and he didn't trust it. He measured the distance between his hairline and the bridge of his nose with his forefinger and thumb and brought the results down in front of his eyes where he could see it. It didn't look like it had progressed. In his dreams, he always had a nice, full head of hair. Of course, in his dreams he could skateboard, too. In reality, he'd never been on a skateboard in his life. He had trouble keeping his balance on a moving city bus when all the seats were taken, let alone a little slab of wood mounted on wheels going 40 miles per hour down a steep hill. Satisfied that his hairline hadn't receded during the past twenty-four hours, he climbed into the shower to ready himself for another day in the real world.

Kyle was twenty-three years old and though he still had most of his hair, he knew he was following his dad's lead and would probably be mostly bald by thirty. He had accepted this fact long ago and had no ill feelings toward his dad for passing along that particular gene. He was not vain, at least not in the real world. But of course, when dreaming, one can be whomever they want to be and do whatever they want to do. Flying was Kyle's favorite thing to do.

Looking through his dream journal, which he usually did at least two or three times per week, he was able to keep tabs on the different types of dreams he had each night. At least the ones he could remember. That was the first hurtle he had to climb when learning of this…hobby…was about the best word for it; the art of controlling one's lucid dreams. Kyle wasn't quite in full control yet, but he felt he was getting there. It took lots of disappointment and patience to get as far as he had gotten. But he was so intrigued with the idea from the start that he didn't let the failures frustrate him. Two years later, all that patience was starting to pay off.

Kyle's interest in dreams had been pure happenstance. Out of boredom, he had read an article about lucid dreams and the benefits of learning to control them from a *Ladies Home Journal*, of all places, while sitting in the waiting room of the dentist's office. He wasn't in the habit of reading women's magazines, but it had been the only magazine within reach and he didn't feel like searching the three little end tables scattered about the waiting room for a *Sports Illustrated*. He'd read the entire article twice by the time he finally heard his name called out by the dental assistant.

Some people remember their dreams more naturally than others. Kyle had fallen somewhere toward the lower end of the middle, occasionally recalling an entire dream the following morning, sometimes remembering bits and pieces, but more often than not, remembering nothing. It took him six months before he began remembering enough of them to start his dream journal. Each night he had gone to bed during that time, he verbally reminded himself as he fell asleep, repeating the reminder over and over like a mantra, to remember his dreams. After all, what good is having a great time in your dreams if you can't recall the experience later? It would be like sleeping through a movie, or the Super Bowl, or sex. How do you know you had a good time if you can't remember it?

So, being able to remember his dreams was the first obstacle. The next step had been simply recognizing the fact that he was in a dream. One needs to train themselves to do periodic reality checks during the day so that it becomes habit. Once the habit is formed, it will continue in their sleep. And if you do a reality check and see a green dog run by or notice that your car is nicer than you ever remember it being, then you are probably dreaming. But just realizing you are dreaming isn't enough to control your dreams. Kyle had spent the week following his visit to the dentist's office surfing the Internet and all its vast resources for information about controlling lucid dreams.

His next step was to go out and buy a watch, one that he could set to beep every hour on the hour. While trying to train himself to remember his dreams as he fell asleep each night, he would perform an hourly reality check during his waking hours. Throughout the day, each time his new watch beeped, he took a moment to look around and notice that he was *not* dreaming. As long as his co-workers weren't all sporting orange Mohawks or his car was still the same old beat-up Dodge, he knew he was in the real world. Then each night, he left his watch next to the alarm clock on the bedside table. About a year after he began this practice, he started occasionally hearing his watch while in a dream and would stop to make a reality check. The first time this happened, he noticed that his girlfriend had her arm around him as they walked downtown. He had instantly snapped awake, saying out loud, "I'm dreaming!" The only problem was that his excitement from the sudden realization that he was aware that he was dreaming had accelerated his adrenalin enough to wake him up. He had read in his research that this was likely to happen but had convinced himself that it wouldn't happen to him because he was informed and ready for it. He was a little disappointed when his reading's prediction came true, but the event was still enough to begin a new chapter in his dream journal and keep him motivated to maintain his training and patience. He knew it had been a dream. It was the only time he could remember being happy that he didn't actually have a girlfriend.

* * *

Over the following months, Kyle learned to stay calmer after recognizing that he was dreaming. This also helped with the number and clarity of the dreams he was able to remember. The next step had been the most fun, beginning to control his dreams.

There were more frustrations similar to the first realization. Kyle still wasn't remembering his dreams every night. There were many gaps between the entry dates in his journal. Nine or ten times a month was doing pretty good. So when he excited himself awake during a particularly good dream, it might be another week before the opportunity to try to return to it arrived. It took three months before he finally accepted the fact that Carly Simon really did want to sleep with him. In order for something to happen in your dream, you have to be able to convince yourself that it could happen…at least while dreaming. The first three times Kyle was wooed into his own bedroom by Carly, she kept turning into girls he had known in college about the same time she started stripping off her flower print sun dress. Deep down, he knew someone like Carly Simon wouldn't have the time of day for a nobody like him, let alone lay on his bed in anticipation of passionate love making. But he kept telling himself, night and day, that anything was possible in a dream. That was the whole point of a dream, wasn't it? To be able to experience things first hand that reality could never offer.

Then one night, Carly remained Carly and there she was, lying on his bed, arms seductively reaching out for him, her wide, sensual mouth slightly open. "Remain calm," Kyle reminded himself out loud in his dream. He reached out and could actually feel her soft, copper skin. She looked just like she did on her *Playing Possum* album cover, wearing a skimpy black negligee, her youth frozen in time. He had awakened the moment he started to crawl into bed next to her…admonishing himself as he awoke for not staying calm enough to ride out the dream. It was still another month or so before he finally got to ride that dream to his imagined conclusion. Since then, there were a few entries in the journal that read something like "Goldie Hawn - my room" and "Uma Thurman and Daryl Hannah – Chinese Garden." Of course, Goldie hadn't aged a bit since *Butterflies Are Free*, and Uma was wearing a short-haired black wig, while Daryl wore a black patch sporting the Red Cross logo over one eye. But he remembered the dreams, recorded them in his journal, and wondered why the whole world wasn't making better use of the twenty-two years the average person spends sleeping during their life.

Believe it or not, however, what Kyle had recently discovered he enjoyed even more than making love to gorgeous, young stars of the stage, was flying. This involved a particular nightmare of his when he had been young. Every summer, his family went on a two-week long driving tour of one part of the country or another. Florida one year, Mount Rushmore, the Grand Canyon, Disneyland, on others. When he was eleven years old, they went driving through the Rocky Mountains. They hiked the Tetons and went to Yellowstone and saw a Broncos game. One day while out driving around exploring the area, they took a wrong turn and found themselves climbing a remote mountain road too skinny for two cars to pass and with no guard rail between the road and a steep drop down the mountain's side. His mother had been visibly terrified until they found a place wide enough to turn around and finally made it back down to the main road. And even at that slightly widened spot, his dad made him and his mom get out of the car while he maneuvered at ten-point turn…just in case.

Kyle often had nightmares over the next couple of years in which the car plunged over the edge whenever he attempted to turn around, sometimes with just his dad in the car, leaving him and his mom stranded on the mountain side, sometimes with all three of them still in the car. He eventually grew out of the nightmare, but he had never forgotten it.

Now Kyle revisited a similar stretch of road, with a few custom-made alterations to serve his purpose, as often as possible, using it as his runway for liftoff. Once he became comfortable controlling the people he saw and the places he went in his dreams, it was time to start imagining the things he could *do* in his dreams. He could be invisible, for example, or ten feet tall. As long as he recognized that he was in a dream, kept his cool, and told himself that it was possible, he slowly began to believe there was nothing he couldn't do. But once again, just telling himself that he could fly hadn't made it happen.

Even in the make-believe world of dreams, there are still some things that need to be figured out and explained. Exactly how one goes about flying, being one of the more important ones. After a few unsuccessful attempts at flight with wings instead of arms and jumping from buildings instead of mountainous cliffs, he finally convinced himself that he was as light as air and could just ride the wind.

Kyle was walking from the bus stop to work downtown on a crowded city sidewalk when he noticed Phoebe Cates walking toward him wearing the same red bikini she had worn in *Fast Times at Ridgemont High*, still dripping wet, eyes locked on his as she approached. That was when he knew he was dreaming. A moment later, he was standing on that old mountain road, looking out over the same valley his nightmare had continually plunged him into so many years earlier. It was a windy day, the wind coming down off the mountain. Kyle thought about what it would be like to ride that wind out over the valley, to just leap off the edge and glide gracefully back to the Earth a mile or better below. Then he thought doing it would be better than thinking about it and dove over the edge like he was swan-diving off the high board into a pool.

He had awakened immediately after leaping into the air that night, but he kept returning to the dream as often as he could, slowly altering his surroundings to suit his needs and desires, patiently training himself to get used to the idea that he could fly. Mostly, he practiced remaining calm, tried not to act excited in his dreams even if he was feeling it. Then one night in his dream, he decided he needed speed, a good running start to get air born. To date, he had flown off his latest version of the mountain on a motorcycle, a bicycle, roller skates, and a convertible, but his favorite tool was the skateboard because it was the only one that he had never actually experienced in the real world and the thrill of speeding down the mountain road on it was almost as exhilarating as the flying itself.

His frustration came in staying air born. Because he had decided he needed momentum for liftoff, he often had trouble sustaining flight over time. It was only recently that he had begun to accept the idea that he could launch from anywhere, even from the ground. But it wasn't foolproof. He was yet to conclude a flying dream on his own terms. So far, each had ended with him falling out of the sky or unable to lift off from a treetop. Then he would awaken feeling a little cheated and frustrated.

But he hadn't given up. Last night he had landed three times and taken flight again before falling out of the sky. He was definitely making progress. His alarm clock had manifested itself into his dreams as a flashing red light. When flying, it appeared as a pterodactyl. For whatever subconscious reason, he frequently saw pterodactyls flying through the sky with him. He assumed it was a compromise his mind had made. If he could fly, then they could exist. But as soon as one started flashing red, he knew his alarm clock was sounding off back in the real world and it was time to wake up. One morning, after spending the night with Julia Roberts, he woke up to the alarm clock to find Julia still lying next to him in his bed. He was about to wake her and ask how she was still there when one of her bare breasts started flashing red and he suddenly woke up again, this time alone.

Another reason why Kyle now preferred flying over spending the night with sexy movie stars was that he had recently met someone. Kyle worked in accounts payable for the Minnesota Department of Transportation. He checked the math on payments being sent out by MinDOT, making sure the owner of the mailbox that had been knocked over by the city snow plow was only getting reimbursed $50.00 instead of $500.00; tires flattened by potholes only received $75.00, not $750.00; things like that. Most of his day was spent on the ten-key, double checking the arithmetic on payments and invoices of all kinds before they got sent out. It was boring work, but the pay was sufficient, the benefits were good, and the promise of advancement was all but guaranteed through time

About a week after Lisa Styles had started working from the desk next to his, he had been striding down Hollywood Boulevard and ran into Laura Prepon. But when he got her down into Eric Foreman's basement, she morphed into Lisa Styles. The confusion woke Kyle up instantly. The next day at the DOT, he asked Lisa if she'd sit with him during lunch in the cafeteria.

Lunch turned out to be too short and they had agreed to pick up their conversation about dreams again over drinks after work. Lisa, it turned out, was one of those people that almost always remembered her dreams, always had since she was a child. But she had never heard of lucid dreams and had no idea one could learn to control them. The concept had fascinated her as much as it had Kyle and she wanted to hear all about his experiences and how he had managed to achieve what control he had. He told her about his journal and the flying and many other adventures he had experienced, although he neglected to mention all the stars he had slept with.

"So, you think you can teach me to fly?" Lisa asked, raising a finger toward the bartender.

Kyle drained his glass of beer to keep up then swiveled on his stool to face her. The bartender arrived on the other side of the counter and Kyle held up two fingers. After the bartender landed two bottles of Corona on the counter and replaced each of their empty glasses with clean ones, Kyle said, "Easily. You've already got the hardest part down, being able to remember your dreams. Now all you have to do is recognize a dream when you see one and get used to the idea that anything can happen."

"Anything?" she asked, raising an eyebrow teasingly. "So what else have you been doing in your sleep beside flying and winning NBA Championships?"

Kyle knew she was teasing, maybe even getting a little drunk after their four or five beers, but he felt himself blushing anyway, more due to her mischievous tone when she asked the question than the question itself.

"You have, haven't you!" she said, holding her mouth open in animated shock and surprise while poking his arm when he didn't answer right away.

"Well," Kyle stammered. "I haven't got complete control yet," he said, trying to dance around the question.

"That's okay," Lisa smiled. "We all need our secrets. Besides, it's only a dream, right?"

"But they seem so real," Kyle said. He was remembering very vividly his dream from the previous night when Lisa had stretched out on Eric Foreman's couch and told him to get his scrawny little butt over there. It had been in Laura Prepon's voice though. He hadn't actually spoken much to Lisa until lunch earlier that afternoon. But now, here in the bar, her voice was quickly growing on him and he felt like he'd known her for years. While looking into Lisa's intense, green eyes, he knew, at least for a while, his days as a Hollywood stud were probably over.

Lisa was the first person Kyle had talked about his new hobby with. He didn't have a lot of friends. He spent most evenings at home alone, reading fiction; Stephen King, Bentley Little, John Saul, Christopher Moore. He was a fan of dark fiction and suspense. Two months ago, he had taken sick leave for a week and read the entire *Harry Potter* collection for the first time, all seven books, back-to-back-to-back. It had been the most exciting, adventurous, and cheapest vacation he had ever taken. In his dreams that week, he *was* Harry Potter. He had already made plans to take a *Lord of the Rings* vacation as soon as he built up some more sick leave time, but that one was only four novels long and he calculated that adding a couple of days to a weekend would probably be enough. Still, he was looking very forward to it. Currently he was perusing through the Bentley Little collection of horrors.

"We should go get something to eat," Lisa said. "I wasn't planning on staying out this late after work, but I am mesmerized by your dreams. How's Applebee's sound? You up for it?"

Kyle was, of course, and over a shared bottle of red wine and baby back ribs, he related to Lisa all the different methods and techniques he had tried or read about in his quest to assume control of his lucid dreams. It was just after 10pm when they walked out of Applebee's into the night.

"Are you okay to drive home?" Kyle asked.

"Yeah, we finished off the wine over an hour ago. I'm fine," she assured him with a wink. "Those last two cups of coffee have taken hold. How about you? You need a ride?"

Kyle knew what his dreams tonight were going to be about, whether he remembered them in the morning or not. He didn't drink much, only on occasion and only socially. He wasn't sure what effect the alcohol would have on his dreams or his ability to remember them, but he was fairly anxious to find out. "I'm fine, too," he told her. "So, guess I'll see you tomorrow at work."

"Unless we meet tonight in our dreams," she replied in that same mischievous voice, as though she had been reading his thoughts.

"That would be called *dreamscaping*," Kyle said, hoping she couldn't see him blush in the dark parking lot. "Although some people believe that is actually possible, I'm not one of them."

"But you said anything is possible in your dreams."

"We could certainly dream we are together," he explained, feeling a little guilty about the fact that he already had. "But as far as sharing the same dream at the same time, that would probably involve some sort of telepathy which is something way out of my league, if it is possible at all."

"Well, I am going to start my own dream journal tonight," Lisa said. "I'll let you know if you make an appearance."

Then she rolled up on her toes and gave Kyle a quick peck on the cheek and turned toward her car with a final wave his direction. Kyle didn't move until she had unlocked her car and climbed in behind the wheel. He wanted to remember everything for his dreams that night. Her flowing blond hair, the way it rested on her shoulders, the tight corners of her lips, her green eyes, the smooth curves of her youthful, trim body. At that moment, as she turned and waved while walking away from him in reality, the feel of her soft lips still fresh on his cheek, Lisa looked more beautiful to Kyle than any of the Hollywood starlets he had invited into his dreams.

Kyle made the short drive home without incident and went straight to bed.

1422 AD

The Lakota Sioux were losing their battle, losing their land, and losing far too many lives in the process. The Apache of the West had invaded their hilly wetlands without warning and had already done more damage in the first two weeks of this unexpected war than the Lakota thought they could return from. The six remaining Shaman of the eight Lakota Tribes were now meeting in the far eastern side of their territory, safe from the advancing warrior Apache tribes for the time being, but they knew their time was growing short. They sat around a large fire and began the ritual of communicating with the spirit world, a world of gods and demons.

Usually when reaching out to the spirit world, it was only one or two Shaman seeking the knowledge to heal the sick or the wounded. It was dangerous reaching out for the warring spirits, but this was their only chance, their last chance, to save their land, their people, their history, and their pride.

The Apache had attacked two of their western tribes in the middle of the night, killing the majority of their warriors while they slept, along with many of the innocent women and children bedding in the same tepees. They were a merciless people when it came to war. Their land in the west was drier and more barren than the land of the Lakota and they had decided that they needed to take it for their own.

The six Shaman created symbols on the ground with colored sand by the light of the fire and began chanting ancient verses known only to them that had been handed down through the generations and rarely used but never forgotten.

The heat inside their tepee intensified as the fire began to grow tall on its own, reaching for the air coming through a small hole at the top. The grains of colored sand in the symbols on the floor in front of them began to swirl and rise next to the growing flames. The crackle of the burning wood increasing, almost drowning out the sound of their continued chants.

With their arms raised to the heavens, their heads facing downward, and their eyes closed as they chanted more loudly to be heard over the fire, the Shaman did not see the spirit taking form in the center of the fire, but they felt his presence as he arrived and knew that he had answered their call. The fire died low once again and the colored grains of sand dropped back to the earth as the Shaman raised their heads and gazed cautiously upon the Demon they had summoned to help them save their race.

"I know why you have summoned me", the Demon said in the ancient language of the Lakota still known only by the Shaman that had called for him. "I will save your families and your land, and you will worship me. I will save your women and children and you will give me a woman to make a child. When that child has seen 17 winters, he will be made Chief and your people will be his people. Say it to be true and it will be done. Stain the honor of your word and your people will be none."

The Shaman knew there would be a price to pay for the magic needed to save their nation. They were prepared to agree to any terms in order to free their people from certain death. The Apache were strong and many and ruthless. Without the Demon's help, the outcome was easily foreseen. They themselves were old, the youngest of them having seen eighty winters. Each of them knew they weren't long of this world and had already given years of their teachings and knowledge to their sons and grandsons who would replace them when they died. But a promise to hand over leadership of their people to the son of a Demon of War had unknown future consequences and had not been a price they had considered.

The Shaman realized, of course, that there would be no future at all if they refuse. There would be no more Lakota. The price had to be accepted and the agreement was made.

The next day, the Apache warriors fell back and retreated to their own land. Many were falling in their tracks as they went, gasping for air, clutching their stomachs, and falling on their own arrows held out in front of them as they fell. Those that survived took back to their chiefs the story of a great disease that had overcome them as they moved deeper into Lakota territory. They told their chiefs that the land was cursed and that they should look to the west and get far away.

The Lakota Nation would survive. The Demon had kept his part of the bargain and the time had come for the Shaman to honor their payment. The Tribal Chief sent his only daughter, Chumani, into the tent of the Demon. The next day, the Demon returned to the spirit world. Nine months later, Chumani gave birth to a son.

2016 AD

Lisa and Kyle began eating together in the cafeteria every day at lunch, mostly talking about their dreams, but before a month had passed, they'd begun dating. And it was another month after that when Kyle was able to re-confirm that, despite how much he enjoyed sleeping with women in his dreams, the real thing was unmistakably better.

"So was it as good as in your dreams?" Lisa asked. Her smile told Kyle that she had just come to the same conclusion that he had.

"Better," he said, kissing her lightly on her forehead. "Much, much better."

Lisa's progress in controlling her dreams had moved along quite a bit faster than Kyle's had. Her dream log, though she hadn't allowed Kyle to actually read it yet, was more like a diary with daily entries. Kyle was still lucky to log four entries in a week. But his control had vastly improved. He had now mastered the art of flight.

In one of his dreams shortly after they had officially become an item, Lisa had asked him to teach her to fly and in doing so, had instilled in him the confidence he needed to believe in himself. Taking her hand, he performed a dream spin, a technique he had developed to change the scenery in his dreams. During the spin, he simply imagined where he would be when he came out of it, and voila, there he be. He transported himself and Lisa, still holding hands, from his bedroom to the edge of the same cliff that had been in his original nightmare when he was eleven. The road was unpaved and the trees a bit sparser so high up near the timberline, but he didn't need a runway on that day, or any day since. He was Peter Pan and Lisa was Wendy Darling. All he needed was to know that he could do it, to have confidence. Lisa believed in him and he wasn't about to let her down. He and Lisa had leaped over the edge of the mountain together and flown hand in hand for what seemed like an entire day. They flew out of the hills and over a dessert before reaching the Grand Canyon a few minutes after leaving Minnesota. Not long after that, they were out in the Pacific watching whales spout fountains of water out of their blow holes. They dove into the water, scattering a school of minnows and circled an ancient sunken pirate ship before breaking out of the water and soaring off into the sky again, still holding hands. They saw Stonehenge and the Great Pyramids of Giza standing tall behind the mystical Sphinx. Finally, they landed on his front porch back in Duluth and walked inside his house and made love again. That night, it seemed a whole new dream world had made itself available to Kyle. It was that night that he realized he could truly do anything he wanted in his dreams, limited only by his own imagination.

"I agree," Lisa said, rolling back on top of Kyle in his bed. "That was even better than my night with Brad Pitt," she said, kissing his nose. "I wish we could dream together though. I still can't seem to convince myself that I can do anything supernatural."

"You'll get there," Kyle replied. "Just don't give up. You're a natural. It took me more than a year to get as far as you've gotten in just a few months. Besides," he added with a chuckle, "some of the things you just did here in the real world felt pretty supernatural to me."

"I'm serious," she said, with a playful pout. "I want to fly. I want to visit Paris. I want to go to the moon!"

Kyle had told Lisa about their journey around the world together in his dream. That had been the same night that she had first begun to remain in her dreams once she recognized that she was dreaming. Her excitement the next day after telling Kyle of her achievement had waned dramatically when he reciprocated with his most recent experience.

"All you need to do is reason with yourself that you can do it, have confidence in yourself."

"But even though I know it's a dream, I still also know that people can't fly," she said.

"And when Brad Pitt arrived at your house, how did he know who you were?"

"I'd written him a letter asking him to come," she said, knowing Kyle would not be offended that the letter hadn't been addressed to him. Although their dream journals were always conveniently out of sight whenever either of them visited the other's home, they had pretty much related to each other most of the contents within them. They understood the difference between dreams and reality and had made a promise to each other never to be jealous of anything that might happen in a dream. It's only a dream, after all, one's imagination running away with itself. Kyle had even told her about his stint as a Hollywood stud, although he hadn't let on to the regularity that it had occurred before discovering how to fly.

"Next time you try to fly in your dream, I'll be there. I'll tell you that you can do it. I'll show you that you can do it. You know I can, so watch me fly in your dream. Then you'll know that people can fly and you can chase me through the air."

"It would still be better if you could really be there," she said.

"Nothing is real in your dreams. It feels real, but it's not. Try telling yourself that even though people can't fly in reality, they can in dreams. Since you are now aware in your dreams, you can reason that you can fly *because* it's a dream."

"Well, last night I jumped off the high board at a swimming pool at least ten times and hit the water every time."

"Ahh," Kyle said, "I see the problem. You are still giving yourself an out. In case you fall, you know you'll be safe hitting the water. That's a sign that you don't have confidence in yourself yet. Try it with a pool of sharks below you and see if you don't stay in the air a while." Then, looking at the alarm clock next to his bed, "We need to get ready for work. You want the shower first?"

"No. You go ahead. I need to sulk for a minute."

"Don't worry," Kyle said, throwing off the covers and sitting up. "You'll get there. Don't give up."

She grabbed Kyle's arm as he started to rise and pulled him back toward her, their eyes inches apart. "I think I'm falling in love with you, you know," she said softly, searching his eyes for approval.

"I've already fallen for you," he replied.

They kissed one more time, as passionate a kiss as Kyle had ever experienced, and then he climbed out of bed feeling a warmth in his heart he had never known existed. A few months ago, he might have disagreed, but this morning he was sure, reality was definitely better than dreams.

1455 AD

Otaktay, the son of a chief's daughter and a Demon of War, had been made Chief of the Lakota nation as promised when he had turned 17. Unfortunately, he had proven to be more like his dad than his mom. As a child, he learned easily, but proved time and again that obedience was not of his nature. His grandfather, Chief Wambleeska, had tried to instill into Otaktay the morals and traditions of the Lakota people, but the boy did not seem to care about the past. At age ten, he had already killed many animals for the sake of the kill instead of the need for the food or the skins. By age fifteen, he had raped a few women for want of their bodies rather than love. He had already learned by then that there would be no consequences for his actions. He had a destiny to be Chief of the Lakota. Though he had never seen his father's face, he had spoken with him many times in his sleep. He was aware of the deal that had been made with the elder Shaman and he understood that made him above the Lakota law. The promise had to be honored and Otaktay would be Chief if the Lakota wanted to survive.

At the age of sixteen, Chief Wambleeska sent Otaktay into the northern territory of the wilds to live off the land for two cycles of the moon, telling him it was a part of his teachings in preparation of his promised destiny of becoming the nation's Chief, but secretly hoping he would meet his death from the fury of a mountain lion or the hunger of a black bear.

2016 AD

Summer in northern Minnesota was a time of celebration and outdoor fun. Usually by Halloween, the first blanket of snow moved in from Canada, the skies grew gray, often hiding the sun from view for a full month at a time, and despite the comforts and advantages of modern technology, survival became the objective of the year-round residents. Many of the elderly ran away to Arizona or Florida for the worst of the winter months, but those without retirement benefits were left to brave out the cold and shovel their way to spring.

It was the first week of September, the air becoming crisper and the northern winds just beginning to bite, but Kyle was living with a new lease on life. His relationship with Lisa had instilled in him a warmth that even the tyrannical winds sweeping in from Canada could not clout. But even though Kyle's reality had vastly improved over recent months, he still loved his time in the world of dreams as much as he ever had.

Flying had become routine in his dreams. He no longer used his old mountain road backdrop to induce a liftoff. He simply shot into the air the same way he had remembered Superman doing on the retro cable channel every Saturday morning when he'd been growing up. He had even been Superman on many occasions, foiling the misguided evils of various criminals of Duluth, but it was from Lisa Styles instead of Lois Lane that he got his inspirations of heroism from.

To cap off each summer in Duluth, the city had a big Labor Day festival in the city's central park. It was a day to spend shopping at the little, wooden booths that lined the sidewalks where locals sold their artistic creations and stuffing yourself on foot-long hot dogs and deep-fat fried bananas on a stick. There were three-legged races for the couples and treasure hunts for the kids. At dusk was an extravagant fireworks display and at midnight they rolled in a large white backdrop to show an outdoor movie for the entire family. This year it was *Fantasia*, the original one from 1940. Kyle and Lisa had joined the gala mid-afternoon and stayed all the way through to the end of the movie.

Most nights they still slept in their respective homes, but on weekends and holidays, as was the case tonight, they usually went back to Kyle's house on the lake that his parents had left him in their will. The subject of Lisa moving out of her apartment and in with Kyle hadn't yet come up between them, but the thought had certainly crossed each of their minds. Their relationship to this point still had that *'too good to be true'* feel about it and each were hesitant to take the next step thanks to imperfect pasts, afraid that at any moment the bottom could fall out. But in truth, neither had ever been happier in their lives.

In the dream world, Lisa had learned to fly but was still having trouble commanding her surroundings. She said she got dizzy whenever trying the dream spin technique and she didn't always come out of it where she had intended to be and sometimes even spun herself awake. But she often had Kyle's company in her dreams and even though she knew it was her own imagination doing all the work, she usually asked the dream Kyle to take her places she wanted to go in order to get there and they would fly off together, hand in hand, to the different destinations of her choosing.

Kyle had been just about everywhere he had explored on Google Earth and everyplace he could remember reading about or seeing in the movies. He'd even visited his own version of Mars after he and Lisa had rented *Total Recall* from Netflix one night. Nevertheless, he was running out of ideas in his conscious mind and lately in his dreams, he'd simply have fun with whatever situation his subconscious had landed him in as soon as he noticed he was in a dream. The novelty of flying had worn off as the challenge to achieve it had diminished, but the dreams still seemed as real as ever and its world remained a constant marvel.

It was after two in the morning when Kyle and Lisa finally arrived at his house, both exhausted from an active, fun filled day. They had each requested, and been granted, Tuesday off from work so they weren't worried about having to wake up early. After making love in the real world once, they quickly drifted off to sleep, each silently acknowledging that it probably wasn't going to be the last time that they were intimate together that night.

At some point during his sleep, Kyle realized he was wearing a dark blue wizard's gown covered with the same yellow stars and silver slivers of moon that Mickey had worn in *Fantasia* while ordering the multiple broom splinters to magically do his chores for him. It was his own body in the robe, however, his own hand that waved the wizard's wand to and fro, causing the miniature broomsticks to dance back and forth as they filled their pails with water.

Then suddenly the scene changed. He was still wearing the robe and still held the wand in his hand at his side, but the air had grown thick and dark and a volcano was erupting off in the distance in front of him, spewing out burning rocks and fire high into the purple sky. A yellow path that seemed to be made of solid gold appeared at his feet and over the horizon he saw two figures approaching. As the figures neared, he recognized Dorothy merrily skipping toward him, a basket swinging from her arm with Toto bouncing along her side. The conflicting vision of the angry volcano and the happy Dorothy confused Kyle and he just stood there waiting for the classic children's characters to reach him as they skipped along the Yellow Brick Road in his direction.

Then, as real as life, Dorothy stopped in front of him and smiled. Even Toto appeared to be smiling up at him from his feet.

"So," Dorothy said, in a voice that sounded ready to break out in song at any moment. "Are you a good witch or a bad witch?"

Although he had thoroughly enjoyed the fantasy of *The Wizard of Oz* when he had been a young lad, he had been sorely disappointed when watching it again for the first time many years later as an adult. Possibly aided by his knowledge of the too short and too depressing life Judy Garland had gone on to live, the movie had gone the same route as circus clowns. When he had been a small boy, the clowns had seemed colorful and animated and had been his favorite act under the big tent. But as an adult, he could see past their round, red noses and the heavily applied make-up. He saw the sadness in their eyes and the resignation in their postures as they went through the motions of their comedic routines. As an adult, they had looked no happier than the homeless men and women he had seen staking out a busy intersection in town, displaying signs that offered work for food.

With this thought in mind, Kyle looked down at Dorothy and replied, "A bad witch." Then with a wave of the wand, he turned Dorothy into a flying monkey and Toto into a frog. The monkey flew off into the dark sky and the frog hopped quickly after it trying to follow from the ground, still barking like the dog he had been moments before. And Kyle was once again alone in front of the raging volcano.

At first, Kyle thought he would just spin out of there and go…where? He couldn't decide. The active volcano discharging its streaks of orange and red high into the dark sky had an ominous feel to it. Or maybe he'd just been reading too many Bentley Little books lately. But he could feel the heat emitted by the volcano on his face. The shiny golden road at his feet faded to a distasteful, dull brown. A shiver went through his spine and he tried a little harder to think of someplace else to go. He was fully aware of the fact that he was dreaming, knew he could take control at any given second and escape the depressing scene before him but he felt rooted to the ground, unable to move.

Even now, as he was becoming an old hand at controlling his lucid dreams, there were still numerous dreams in which he simply went with the flow and rode it out to where ever it lead him, playing the spectator of his subconscious imagination. He didn't control everything that happened in his sleep, and in fact, sometimes found it more exciting not to. He assumed that was what he was doing at the moment when words he didn't understand escaped his lips and his arm began to raise, aiming the wand at the fiery mountain. He continued to speak words that sounded like nonsensical gibberish to his ears, but he seemed to sense a kind of rhythm to them. It made him feel powerful inside…and a little afraid.

The orange and red fire spewing forth from the inner depths of the volcano suddenly stopped and the mountain appeared to be shifting into a new form. It reminded him of the scene in *Fantasia* that he had seen earlier that evening in the park, when the demon comes alive to rule the night. He had thought that scene a little much for some of the younger children scattered about the audience; thought it would cause more than a few nightmares that night. But Kyle hadn't had a nightmare in longer than he could remember. In fact, since he had learned to control his dreams, he had even tried to initiate one a time or two after reading a good horror story by Stephen King or more recently, Bentley Little. But the fact that he was aware that he was only dreaming prevented him from ever being able to scare himself.

Just as the wings began to unfold from the mountain side as they had in *Fantasia*, the slight breeze that had felt hot against his face shifted and the air began swirling around him, his wizard robe billowing up in all directions. Then there was a loud "POP" and the entire scene changed. The wind, the dark sky, and the volcano were gone. He was back on his old mountain top with the unpaved road and the trees that struggled for air. He looked over the edge of the mountain side but instead of the lush, green valley that had always been there before, he saw a large river running through what looked like the remains of a forest that had been destroyed by fire. The waters of the river were blood red. Then looking down the dirt road to his right, he saw the creature.

Kyle's heart skipped a couple of beats, his adrenaline surged, and he awoke, Lisa still sleeping soundly in his bed next to him. He was still awake when the alarm clock sounded an hour and a half later.

1475 AD

It had been twenty years since Otaktay had become Head Chief of the Lakota nation. Word had spread from tribe to tribe throughout the west that the Lakota had a demon son for a chief so no other nation or tribe had challenged them for their lush land since the retreat of the Apache thirty-eight years earlier. The original six Shaman that had made the deal with the War Demon had long since gone to the spirit world themselves and passed on their wisdom to their now aging sons.

For the most part, Otaktay had solely focused on his own wants and desires, leaving the tribe to govern themselves without his interference. He bedded all the young women for a full cycle of the moon when they turned sixteen before turning them loose to their adult lives. He required all food, gathered and hunted, to be brought to him first and he would take what he wanted and give the rest to the tribe. But no one went hungry and the young girls began to accept their time with Chief Otaktay as an initiation they all had to go through in order to enter their adulthood.

But of course, after twenty years of getting whatever he wanted, Otaktay was getting bored. He called upon the Shaman of each tribe and told them to prepare for war. The land to the west that he wanted to take would not benefit the Lakota nation in any way and the Shaman quickly realized that Chief Otaktay was planning this war for no other reason than because he could, because he had decided he wanted to. Warriors, women and children would die. Killing for nothing to gain was not the Lakota way. And trade with the neighboring nations would forever cease.

The Shaman, getting together without Chief Otaktay after getting told of the Chief's plans, all agreed that this would be a senseless and wasteful war. They were aware of the deal that had been made almost forty years earlier, but felt they had to prevent this war from happening. And the only way to do that would be to remove Chief Otaktay from power.

The discussion of assassinating the Chief was brief and quickly discarded. They feared that killing the son of the War Demon would certainly end up no better than killing their own people. A prison seemed to be the only answer, but no prison they could think of would be enough to hold Otaktay who would simply summon his True Father and bring a new wrath down on their tribe.

The youngest of the Shaman, the only grandson among the group of sons of the six Shaman that had made their pact with the war demon, told the others of an ancient story, of a ritual his grandfather had related to him about sucking the spirit, or the soul, out of a human and placing it into a talisman that is then buried under stone and forever locked away from the mortal world and left unable to communicate with other spirits or demons. It was not a spell that could work against a demon, but Chief Otaktay was born of a human mother and therefore, having nothing to lose that they wouldn't be losing anyway by doing nothing, the Shaman decided to reincarnate the ancient spell.

It was the daughter of the grandson who was turning sixteen in a day and was going to be spending her next month with the Chief receiving her initiation into womanhood. While the Chief slept with her at his side, she was asked to cut a lock of his hair and bring it to her father, along with a feather from his headdress. The Shaman then created a talisman and began the ritual to lock away forever the spirit of their evil Chief and maintain a peaceful relation with their neighboring nations.

2016 AD

I think I had my first nightmare since I was a kid last night," Kyle told Lisa, while they were sipping their morning coffee in his kitchen. "It was like a weird mix between *Fantasia* and *The Wizard of Oz*, or something like that. I don't remember much of it anymore. I didn't write anything down when I woke up, but I remember being glad I was awake. I just can't remember exactly why."

"You probably had one too many of those banana things on a stick yesterday," Lisa replied, smiling over her mug.

"But I only had one."

"I know," Lisa giggled. "And it was probably one too many. So, what do we want to do with our day off today?"

Kyle put his mug on the kitchen table and walked into the living room, standing in front of the large oriel that looked out over the lake. He felt Lisa's arm snake around his waist as she joined him by his side, staring out at the water.

"Lately I've been thinking about how big this place is for just one person," he said.

"You're not thinking of moving, are you?"

"No," he answered, turning towards Lisa and wrapping both his arms around her waist. Then, looking directly into her eyes, he added, "I was just thinking about how happy I feel every time I wake up and see you lying next to me."

Lisa slid both her arms up around his neck and pulled him close. "I dreamed last night that I lived here," she said, almost in a whisper. "Are you saying that you want to make my dreams come true?"

After making love on the floor of the living room in front of the window facing the lake with the morning sun shining through and warming their naked bodies, they spent the rest of the day making several trips moving everything that would fit into their cars from her apartment into his house… into their house.

"We can rent a U-Haul this weekend and get the bigger stuff," Kyle said, as they carried in their final load of the day. "When is your lease up?"

"A couple more months," she told him. "But I've been there for three years and the landlord is a nice guy. I'll bet if I explain, he'll let me out of it."

"Well, even if he doesn't, this place is already paid for so I can certainly help out if you need it," he assured her.

"I don't deserve you," she said. "But I'm not giving you back. What do you want for dinner?"

"Anything but fried bananas on a stick."

* * *

Kyle found himself walking down the sidewalk of downtown Duluth again, as was often the case in the beginning of his dreams since it was something he usually did five days per week. Lisa was with him at his side. If the semi-truck that was driving by in the street had been making any noise, he might not have recognized that he was dreaming. At least not until after it had passed. They were standing on the street corner waiting for the light to change when it rolled silently by. He could hear others waiting for the light chatting next to him, and he heard the beeping of the walk signal announcing to the blind that it was their turn to cross. But apparently his mind had muted the traffic.

He and Lisa began to cross the street towards the DOT building where they worked after the truck cleared the intersection. It was then that he saw it. Kyle stopped in the middle of the street, unable for a moment to get his feet to move. Standing on the opposite corner was the same creature he had seen on the old mountain road the previous night right before he had snapped awake. It appeared as though it were waiting for them to cross to its side. Kyle had not been able to recall what it had looked like after awakening yesterday. In fact, by the time Lisa had awakened next to him, he had a hard time remembering much of anything from the dream, let alone what had given him the willies. But now, back in dreamland, he recognized it immediately and knew without a doubt that it was the same creature.

Creature was the only word he could come up with for it. It wasn't human, but it was unlike any animal he had ever imagined. It stood erect on two cloven feet; its bowed legs were covered with thick, dark hair that stretched all the way up to its stomach. Its torso appeared scaly like that of a snake, but it had the head of an earless mule and its humanoid arms were far too long, hanging well past its knees. Its hands appeared to end with the talons of an eagle rather than fingers. Its beady, black eyes were rooted on Kyle and finally his feet moved as he instinctively took a step backward. The creature smiled a sinister looking grin and opened its long, wide mule mouth, showing off far too many sharp, pointed teeth.

"Let's get out of here," he said to Lisa, and immediately took her hand in his and performed a dream spin.

But when he came out of the spin, he was alone, Lisa seemingly no longer a part of this

(nightmare)

dream. As he slowly turned around to see where he had landed, he noticed he was out in the middle of the lake behind his house, floating in a canoe that he didn't own. He located his house on the shore and saw Lisa standing in the oriel, blankly looking his direction but as though she couldn't see him there at all. Then he saw the creature sidle up next to her and he started frantically using the oar he discovered he was holding to paddle quickly to shore.

The only sound was his own heart pumping wildly in his chest. Noticing that he couldn't even hear the splashing water at his side, he reminded himself that this was only a dream and that he could fly to her if wanted to or even spin himself into the room with her and the creature. Even better, he could just wake up. But then, feeling his panic rise a little more with each stroke of the oar, he briefly wondered why his accelerated adrenaline hadn't already brought him out of his sleep.

As he reached the shore, not taking his eyes from the scene in his upstairs living room window, Lisa appeared to be in a trance, unaware of the

(*monster*)

creature at her side. She continued to stare out into the lake as though in deep thought. The thing by her side, however, was attentively watching Kyle's every move with those beady, black eyes. It stood almost two feet taller than Lisa. It grinned at Kyle when he started running past the large boulder on the shore of the lake and up the hill of his backyard that sloped down into the water and then it turned to face Lisa. Its mouth stretched impossibly wide over her head as though it were about to remove it from her shoulders in a single bite. Slimy drool fell from its lipless mouth and dropped onto her head like a fat, polluted raindrop. Lisa still didn't seem to notice.

"NO-O-O!!" Kyle screamed as he tried to dream spin himself into the house. The sky turned the same dark purple he recognized from the site of the volcano in his dream the previous night and the earth began to shake violently. "NO-O-O!!" he screamed again…

…and he saw Lisa's worried face directly in front of him. She was shaking him vigorously and he felt disoriented and lost. "It's okay," she was repeating over and over again. "It's only a dream. Wake up. You're home. It's okay."

Eyes wild and wide, Kyle looked around the room without raising his head. They were in his bed, in his house, and appeared to be alone. "Real?" he asked.

"Real," she replied, pulling him towards her and hugging him tightly against her chest.

Kyle was sweating, his pillow was drenched. Details of the dream were already beginning to fade. "You're okay?" he asked.

"I'm fine," she assured him. "You were screaming in your sleep. I tried to wake you up but you kept screaming and I was starting to get scared. Do you want to talk about it?"

Kyle told Lisa everything that had happened in the dream. Having been quite the lucid experience and being only freshly awakened from it, he found that he remembered just about everything as if it had really just happened. But now that he was back in the real world, the fear he had felt when experiencing the dream was quickly fading away. It was replaced by curiosity and his enthusiasm for adventure.

"It was actually kind of cool, now that I think about it," he told her, his confidence gradually regaining its strength. "It felt like I was relinquishing control of my dream to that thing but I was about to run in and save you from it when you pulled me out of the dream."

"You scared me when you started screaming. I couldn't get you to wake up at first. You think someone can die in their dreams?" she asked.

"No. Not a chance. Even if that thing had bitten your head off in my dream, it's not really you. It's just an image of you my subconscious mind produced. No harm can come to you in a dream, or to me," he added. "I'll just have to try to remember that next time I have a nightmare. It might at least prevent me from waking you up and scaring you with a scream."

"Well, hopefully there won't be a next time," she said. "You really did scare me. For a minute there, I wasn't sure I could wake you up. And you can't leave me now, not after making me fall in love with you." She thought for a second, and then asked, "You don't think that was your subconscious trying to tell you that you don't want me living here, do you? You know, with the potential beheading and all. I mean, you're glad I am here, right?"

"I've never been happier, love. Like I said, I was the one trying to save you, not the one trying to eat you. Although," he added, with a devilish grin of his own as he moved in closer to her on the bed, "you do taste incredibly delicious. I might just eat you up myself right now." Then he leaned in and started kissing her face, her neck, her shoulder, and he hadn't been lying. She tasted wonderful on his lips. She wrapped her arms around him and they promptly forgot about dreams and nightmares and impossible head-eating monsters.

* * *

A noise somewhere in the house woke Kyle up. He sat up in bed, rubbing the sleep out of his eyes and smiled as he looked at Lisa sleeping peacefully next to him. Then he heard what had awakened him again. It sounded like someone was playing ping pong in the basement. He climbed carefully out of bed so as not to disturb Lisa's sleep and pulled on his robe to go see if a pair of criminals had broken in and gotten sidetracked from robbing them by a quick game of ping pong before making their getaway.

"Tick-tick-tick-tick." The sound grew louder as he descended the stairs. Then just as he was rounding the corner to the game room that opened up to the patio in the backyard in front of the lake, he realized how incredibly unlikely it was that someone would break into his house in the middle of the night for a game of ping pong…and that he was probably dreaming.

Sure enough, as he walked into the large, open room, the ping pong ball was bouncing from one side of the table to the other, being batted back and forth by paddles held by invisible hands, seemingly playing a match on their own. He was about to turn around and head back upstairs to crawl back into bed and decide what he wanted to do with this particular dream when he noticed a spectator of the phantom ping pong match sitting in the shadows of the night on the couch that lined the wall. It was the creature.

Remembering his discussion with Lisa about his nightmare from the previous night, he wasn't afraid of the creature. He knew there was no danger in a dream, to himself or to any of the dream's characters. He walked towards the ugly thing sitting on his couch, its furry legs casually crossed and its oversized, unfeasible head going back and forth following the ball intently as though it were watching the U.S. Wimbledon tennis finals.

"So why are you haunting my dreams?" Kyle asked the creature as he approached.

The ping pong paddles suddenly dropped to the floor and the ball carried into the wall before landing on the carpet after not being returned. The creature shifted its attention to Kyle, but remained silent.

"What are you anyway?" Kyle asked. "Some weird monstrosity from one of my Bentley Little books, or what?"

Kyle was about to think that the creature wouldn't talk, but then it did in a deep, gravelly voice that reverberated against his bones like someone had cranked up the bass too high on their car stereo. It wasn't loud, it wasn't a matter of volume, but he could feel the thing's voice as much as he could hear it. "You like the power you have in dreams, don't you, Kyle. You like to be in control."

"As a matter of fact, I do," Kyle told the creature. "And right now I'd like to get rid of you and move on to something a little less ugly."

Kyle went into a dream spin thinking about Lisa and the first lunch they had shared in the cafeteria of the DOT. That had been another benefit to controlling your dreams. Not only can you experience new things and go new places, but you can also relive all your favorite moments of the past from the real world.

The dim basement faded away and was replaced by the lunch room with its bright florescent lights overhead and the sounds of chatter from his co-workers and silverware tapping against the hard plastic plates. But instead of Lisa sitting across from him at their table, the creature sat in her place, beaming smugly at him as though having just delivered the punch line to a good joke. But there was no humor in the two black marbles it had for eyes.

"You can't shake me that easily," it said.

Kyle went into another spin, this time coming out of it high in the sky, soaring in the wind over the ocean with a couple of pterodactyls...and the creature flying along his side.

"Where're we going?" the creature asked.

Kyle was getting tired of this and tried to wake himself up, but nothing happened. He did another dream spin from the air, a maneuver he'd never tried before but it seemed to work. He found himself back in his home, standing at the foot of his bed looking at Lisa sleeping under the covers.

At least he had assumed it was Lisa. But he was wrong. The covers flew back and the creature was lying in her spot, still displaying that repulsive grin with too many spiky teeth. "Care to join me?" it snarled at Kyle.

Kyle spun out of his bedroom with nowhere in mind. He needed to think, or to stop thinking and organize all the thoughts beginning to push his brain toward overload. This creature was now making him feel uneasy. He remembered when the creature had first spoken, saying something about the power of controlling your dreams. Kyle felt like he was losing control of his and he couldn't figure out why.

He came out of his spin in a small, square room with empty, white walls. He was sitting on a metal fold-up chair in front of a fold-up card table in the center of the room. The only door had a small barred window with no glass. It looked like an interrogation room or a room where a prisoner is allowed to visit with a relative in moderate privacy. There was another chair across the table from Kyle, but it was thankfully empty. The beast was at least for the moment no longer stalking him in his dream and Kyle needed a minute to collect his thoughts.

Kyle slammed his hand onto the table as hard as he could, planting a dimple into its surface from the impact. His hand felt no pain. He was trying to wake himself up. A bare light bulb encased in a wire mesh above the door that hadn't been there when Kyle had first looked around the room started flashing red and Kyle thought *"saved by the bell*" thinking his alarm clock was going off and he'd be waking up any second.

But he didn't wake up.

Instead, the door opened and the creature stepped in. It turned and shut the door, and though it had closed without making a sound, Kyle couldn't help but feel like the creature had somehow just locked him in. The light bulb behind the creature stopped flashing.

In the real world, Lisa reached over Kyle as he slept and turned off the alarm clock. She was feeling a little stiff as a result of all the packing and lifting from the move yesterday. And *she* had only handled the light stuff. But it was back to work today, sore muscles or not. She decided to let Kyle sleep in while she showered and dressed first. Then she could wake him up and he could get ready while she put something together for breakfast. She gave Kyle a loving smile and a kiss on the cheek as he slept and got out of bed to get the day started.

In the dream world, the creature pulled the empty chair out from the table with its long, almost human arms, its talons clicking tauntingly against the metal frame as it grabbed it, and took a seat. It took a moment to look around the room, just as Kyle had done a minute earlier when he had come out of his spin. "Appropriate," it said, turning its emotionless, black eyes back to Kyle.

Kyle felt himself tense up, pushing hard against the pad on the backrest of his chair, and tried to relax, reminding himself that this was only a dream. Although it felt like he was quickly losing control of his dream; that in itself wasn't actually anything new. But the added fact that it felt like control and been turned over to this sadistic looking creature with the deformed mule head; that bothered him.

Kyle couldn't speak. He didn't know if it was because he was too scared and confused all of a sudden to think of anything to say; or if maybe his mouth was currently physically unable to produce sound, his vocal cords having been stripped from his throat at the whim of the impossible creature before him. Kyle tried to spin out of the room. He didn't actually believe he was going to go anywhere and tried to reason with himself that that was why he hadn't when he didn't…but he didn't believe that either. He was somehow being held captive by this obscene creature in his own dream. And he was locked in.

"Power," the creature said, as Kyle tried to focus. "The power is good."

"What power?" Kyle asked, finding he could still talk after all.

"The power to control your reality. To live completely free of obligation and guilt. To live like a king."

"But this isn't reality," Kyle argued. "This is a dream. *My* dream, in case you hadn't noticed. And all I want to know is how to stop finding you in it."

"But you are here now. And I am here," said the creature. "We interact. This is our reality."

"But you aren't real," Kyle reasoned. "You exist only in my imagination."

"You've not felt my power? Have you not already tried to leave here and failed?"

Yes, Kyle had felt its power, and he had also failed every attempt to leave this room, but he refused to believe that this monster had somehow gained control of his dreams. It didn't seem possible, even in the world of dreams where anything is possible, and he wasn't ready to accept it. "I don't understand."

"I could feel you. Your power in my reality is strong. But it *is* my reality," the creature commanded. "Yours is on the other side."

Things can't happen in your dreams unless you first believe that they are possible. Everything Kyle had learned about this stuff had led back to that fact. So how could this be happening? He certainly didn't believe it was possible. Could this all be a self-imposed nightmare? Is this simply another half-hearted attempt to scare himself, except this time he was actually succeeding? *Just calm down*, he thought. *There's got to be a reason for this. There's got to be a way to make it all stop.* "Why are you in my dream?"

"I told you. Because I could feel you. Your spirit called to me and I came. I am the answer to your most desired dreams. I can make you immortal."

"I don't remember inviting you here," Kyle said. "And I have no desire to be immortal, as if that were even an option."

"I fed you the words in front of the volcano," the creature admitted, "and you spoke them aloud and here I am. And now I have an offer for you that you won't be able to refuse. A trade, you might say. But I think you will like the perks."

Kyle didn't think the offer was going to be anywhere near as enticing as the creature seemed to believe it was, but he knew he was going to hear it anyway. He was trying again to spin out of the room but it was like his motor had thrown a cog or something because he couldn't get any rotation going. He just sat there in his chair, shaking a little.

In the real world, Lisa came out of the bathroom cleaned and dressed and sat next to Kyle on the bed. She stared at his slumbering face for a moment, thinking about how lucky they were to have found each other, and leaned in to give him another secret kiss before waking him up. As her face hovered an inch away before she kissed him, she noticed the sweat on his brow. His sideburns were damp and there were a few streaks now visible where salty drops had escaped his brow and skated across his face towards the pillow.

"Kyle?" she said, abandoning the kiss, remembering yesterday when he had needed to be shaken awake. He had been sweating then, too. "Kyle. Time to wake up. Right now, Kyle! Wake up!"

Lisa started shaking him.

In the dream world, the creature explained. "I was in your world once a long time ago. I was powerful there. I can speak to the spirits of the underworld. Take me with you back to your world and I will grant you the power of your dreams in your reality. You can be a king of your race. You can have immortality. And I can avenge my banishment. But in order for me get back, you need to consent to uniting our spirits for the journey."

"And if I refuse to take you with me?" Kyle asked.

"Then you shall remain here until your body dies in your reality. The choice is yours. Take me with you and you will live as a king of kings." The creature then leaned forward and added with a growl, "Stay, and you shall die."

Kyle was right. The offer sucked. He could unleash some demon-type creature on the world and possibly become one himself, or he could waste away in his sleep until his body died of starvation. Even if he opted to stay and Lisa managed to get him to the hospital and hooked up to life support, he'd still be stuck in this nightmare, aware and unable to awaken from a cursed coma. Assuming of course, that what the creature said was not simply Kyle's overactive imagination doing a real number on himself.

Kyle didn't know what to believe at the moment. All he knew for sure was that he should have already wakened up by now. He hoped Lisa wasn't worried about him yet. He didn't want to scare her again the way he had yesterday. He needed to figure this out. Whether anything the creature was trying to tell him was true or not, whether there could possibly be more than one level of reality or this was all just an illusion of his mind, he just wanted to figure it out and get back to Lisa.

In the real world, Lisa brushed away her tears and tried to think of what she should do. She had felt his pulse and it was strong. She could see his chest rise and fall with each breath. His eyes beneath his lids were darting back and forth, signifying that he was in an REM state. He looked at peace, if she ignored the dampness on his face and pillow from sweating. She knew he was dreaming. She was pretty sure the creature he had described yesterday was the cause of his continued slumber. She wanted to call 911 but didn't know what to say. What was she going to tell the officer that answered, that her boyfriend was being held captive in his dream by a monster and they needed to send someone out to wake him up? And then what if they couldn't do it either? Where would they take him? What would they do to him? She didn't know what to do so she waited. Every few seconds, she checked that his chest was still moving up and down and confirmed that his eyes were still active beneath the lids, and repeated his name softly. But mostly she just sat next to him, running a worried hand through his hair, trying to figure out who she could call that might know how to help. Worrying that maybe no one could help at all.

In the dream world, Kyle continued to try to figure out what was going on. "So why do you need me? Why don't you just take me?" he asked the creature.

"Because you can travel from this reality to the next. You can take me to the talisman under the stone. But I need your consent."

"What talisman? What stone? Why can't you just go there yourself?"

"I was once a great Chief of my nation. I saved them from extinction and gave them peace. But when war was needed, they betrayed me and performed a ritual, sucked my spirit from my body and placed it in a talisman and buried it below a great stone. Then they burned my body taking away the home for my spirit. I have waited more than five hundred winters for a life force to come and carry me back to your world."

"Where is this stone that your talisman is buried under?" Kyle asked, more just to keep the thing talking than out of curiosity. He didn't necessarily believe what the creature was saying as fact, but he was groping for anything that might clue him in on how to get out of this nightmare.

"It is close," the creature said. "My spirit has remained trapped all this time, waiting for you. We shall go back to your world as one. We shall remove the talisman from under the stone and place it in the ashes of a soul that has been cleansed by fire. And I will speak to the spirits of the underworld and the ashes will take new form and my spirit will live free once again inside that form. You will then be rid of me but I will grant you the power to do as you wish and to live as you choose before I leave you and avenge my banishment. I will grant to you the secret of immortality for your great service to me."

"Why should I trust you?" Kyle asked.

"You have no choice," the creature answered with a toothy grin. "That is of course, if you ever want to return to her again."

The creature nodded to the wall on his left and Kyle saw Lisa appear out of thin air, sitting in a chair like his own against the wall, but with the same glossed over look in her eyes that she had when standing next to the creature in his living room during his previous dream. Kyle knew it wasn't actually Lisa. But he also knew there was no way he was bringing a monster like this back to life in reality. Kyle had already made his decision, but remained silent. If this thing were speaking the truth, then Kyle had to accept his fate. But if this was indeed just a nightmare gone crazy created by his own imagination, then he had no doubt that Lisa would find a way to wake him from it.

The creature had been right. He had no choice. He could do nothing and decided nothing was what he would do. He needed time, he thought, as he looked longingly at the image of Lisa sitting quietly off to the side. He needed to give Lisa time to figure out how to wake him up. But he knew that wouldn't be enough. He'd have to go back to sleep again eventually and when he did, he would dream. And the creature would still be here waiting for him. No, if this was ever going to end, Kyle had to get back to his reality and find that talisman and destroy it. But his chances of accomplishing that seemed as unlikely as escape presently did from this prison the creature had condemned him to.

"I'll give you two some time to think it over," the creature said.

It got up from its chair and left the room, shutting the door silently behind it as it left, leaving Kyle alone with the image of Lisa. He imagined Lisa back in the real world and wondered if she was trying to wake him up. He wished he could talk with her; tell her he was okay. Or maybe he was just wishing he'd had the chance to tell her good-bye.

In the real world, feeling like she should be trying to do something to help Kyle, though having no idea what that something could possibly be, Lisa pulled a few books out of Kyle's study that he had collected about lucid dreams and brought them back into the bedroom with Kyle. She had called the DOT office and reported that both she and Kyle had gotten sick at the Labor Day festival, probably something they'd eaten, and would not be in to work today but would hopefully be well enough to return tomorrow. She knew her supervisor hadn't believed her, but she didn't care. For the past hour she'd been flipping through the books looking for anything that might relate to what was going on with Kyle but had found nothing that described being unable to come out of one's dream. She was lying next to him on his bed, reading about out of body experiences when her eyes slid slowly closed and she fell asleep.

In the dream world, Lisa was making love to Kyle. But as she looked down at his face, she saw that he was sleeping through her passion and she became aware that she was dreaming. She rolled off of him and stared at him, aware that she was worried about him, aware that he could not seem to wake up in reality, and aware that this was not him in front of her, but merely an image of him that her imagination had produced for the dream.

But what was she doing here? Kyle needed her back in the real world. She shouldn't be sleeping. She should be trying to help Kyle, but she had no clue what she could do. Though she certainly didn't feel like she had been doing him any good from there either, crying and reading useless books. She looked at the dream Kyle and wished she could get to him, *really* get to him, in his dream. She wanted to talk to him and find out what he needed her to do. But that was impossible.

Or was it?

Hadn't she just been reading about people who had left their bodies? Where did they go? What did they do? She couldn't remember. But it made her think. She lay down on the bed next to Kyle and tried to concentrate, not on the dream Kyle next to her, not on the real Kyle sleeping in the real world, but on herself, her real self that was lying next to the real Kyle back in the real world. She imagined her spirit floating out of her body, the way the book she had been reading when she fell asleep described it. The image she was holding onto with every ounce of mental strength she could muster began to fade and grow dark. And then the darkness faded and she was again looking at herself and Kyle lying side by side in bed, but something was different. It took her a moment to realize what it was. She was looking at Kyle *and* herself. And unlike the vision of Kyle that had just faded away, this one was sweating. Looking more closely at herself, she could see where her eyeliner had run a little bit from her earlier tears. Then she realized these weren't images from her dream. She was hovering over her real self. She was looking at her and Kyle sleeping side by side in the real world.

She looked at Kyle and glided slowly over him, hovering above him instead of herself. She stared into his face and imagined herself soaking into the pores of his skin, getting into his head, joining his dream. She could feel his heart beating and the blood surging through his body; she could sense his distraught mind. She could feel his terror. She was sitting in a chair against a wall of a small room. Kyle was before her, sitting in another chair at a table in the middle of the room, looking at her with his mouth open.

Kyle had been staring at the image of Lisa when he saw the life enter her eyes. One moment she was staring blankly at the opposite wall, then she blinked and her eyes returned, wide and confused, but obviously aware. There was a light in her eye that had not been present in any of his previous visions that made her even more beautiful than the dream versions of her that he had been interacting with over the better part of a year.

He didn't know how, but he knew it was really her. Somehow, she had gone looking for him and found him. God, he loved her. But he had to get her out before the creature came back. If it got a hold on her mind too, they might both be imprisoned here forever. Or maybe she had already been trapped by merely coming.

"Lisa?" Kyle whispered.

"Kyle?" she said, as she started to stand up.

"Don't move," Kyle said quickly, putting a finger in front of her mouth telling her to remain quiet. "I don't know when it'll be back, but you can't stay here. You need to go back."

"You're coming with me," she said. "I'm not leaving without you."

"But how? How did you even get here?"

"I'm not sure how any of this works, but you have to come back with me. I can't wake you up."

"But even if I could go back…"

"I know you can," Lisa interrupted. "We just need to believe it and it can happen. You taught me that. It's got to work."

"But even if it does," Kyle started again, "I can't stay awake forever. I'll need to sleep sometime. And when I do, that creature will be waiting for me. It wants me to…"

Kyle stopped and held his breath. He was about to tell Lisa that the creature wanted him to take it back to reality with him. And if he was capable of riding Kyle out of this reality into the next, then maybe he *could* ride Lisa out, if in fact, she wasn't also already a prisoner herself. But then what? Like he said, the creature would just wait for his return. As soon as Kyle fell asleep again, this whole nightmare would start over. Unless…

"Okay," Kyle whispered, quickly deciding what they needed to do. "How can we get out of here?"

"I don't know," Lisa said, tears beginning to well up in her eyes. "I just want you to come back."

She stood and stepped toward Kyle. Kyle didn't stop her this time but also stood, reaching out his arms as she approached. They embraced each other full of emotion and desire, the desire being to leave this place and return to their reality as quickly as possible.

"I love you," Kyle said.

"I love you, too. Now come home with me."

The door opened and the creature stepped in looking a little confused at the sight of Kyle and Lisa embracing. Then as Kyle saw its form losing its distinct edges and start to waver out of focus, he heard it let out a roar that shook every bone in his body. Kyle closed his eyes, closed his mind, and concentrated on the feel of Lisa's body and squeezed her against his own as hard as he could.

Kyle woke up lying on his side, facing Lisa's sleeping form next to him in his bed. Her body suddenly seemed to shimmer a bit, like a mirage on a heated desert highway, and then he saw her eyes open and they immediately filled with tears as she rolled over and hugged Kyle, kissing his face frantically between her words. "We did it! You're back! I love you! I love you!"

Her excitement quickly waned as she remembered what Kyle had said about going back to sleep right before the creature had returned and they had made their miraculous escape. She fell back, giving him room to breathe. "What are we going to do? You can't live the rest of your life without sleeping. What's going on? What is that thing in your dreams?"

"A stupid spirit from some other world that talks too much," Kyle told her. "Come on. We're going to put a stop to it right now."

"What? How? Where are you going?" she called after him, trying to keep up.

Kyle didn't even bother getting dressed first. He threw on his robe as he ran and headed down the stairs and out the patio door into the backyard, Lisa following closely behind him, unwilling to even let him out of her sight until this got resolved.

"I think it's there," he told her, pointing to the large rock by the shore of the lake. "He said it was buried under a stone and was close by. He said he'd been waiting under it for five hundred years."

"What do you mean, buried under the rock? What's down there?" She was even more confused now than she had been when suddenly arriving in Kyle's dream. "Waiting for who?"

Kyle explained about the Chief and the talisman while pushing and pulling at the large boulder with all his might but it wouldn't even budge. He told her how the creature wanted revenge over those that had been responsible for his banishment, but Kyle had gotten the feeling that the creature's idea of who was responsible had not been limited to a handful of relatives of the individuals that had put a stop to his rein on earth. He was after all of them. Kyle believed the creature's blame pretty much included the entire human race.

Kyle ran back up the hill toward the garage, Lisa quickly trailing after him. "Have you got your keys?" he asked her. "Your car is newer and more powerful than mine."

She reached into the pocket of her work slacks and drew out a key ring, tossing it to Kyle who caught them and went inside the garage. He grabbed a coil of extra co-axle cable the satellite guys had left him in case he got a second TV he wanted to hook up and threw it into the back seat of Lisa's mini-van and climbed in. Lisa got in the passenger side.

"I'm only driving to the backyard, but you can have a ride if you want," he said, trying to smile, but failing.

"I'm going where you're going," she replied.

Kyle backed out of the driveway and barely had room to drive the mini-van between his house and his neighbor's as he did a backwards u-turn and backed the vehicle to the top of the hill in his backyard. He grabbed the cable and tied one end around the bumper of the car, the other around the boulder.

"Why don't you climb in and drive while I push," he suggested.

She did, but the rock still didn't budge. It only came up about waist high, but it must have weighed a ton and, if this was indeed the right one, it probably hadn't been moved in more than five hundred years.

Kyle removed the cable. The van wasn't going to get near enough traction on the grass to move this rock, especially pulling up hill.

"I've got another idea," he said, and disappeared back into the house.

A moment later, Lisa saw him driving his own car around the side of the house. Lisa was still sitting behind the wheel of the van.

"Turn it around," he called out his open window to her. "We're going to push it instead of pull it. I push the rock. You push me. Got it?"

He didn't wait for a response. He started slowly down the hill and rested the steel front bumper of his old dodge against the rock. He waved an arm out his window for Lisa to follow. She turned the van around and lined up her bumper to Kyle's trunk, both cars now at an angle that appeared to be steep enough to carry them into the lake if it weren't for the rock. She knew the cars were not going to come out of this unscathed, but figured that would be a small price to pay if it meant not having to worry about whether or not Kyle was going to wake from his sleep every morning.

"Okay," Kyle yelled back from his window. "Push!"

They both stepped on the accelerator and at first nothing happened. But then she started to inch forward. Suddenly both cars lurched toward the lake as the rock finally released its ancient hold on the earth. She slammed on her breaks as she saw Kyle continue forward a few more feet and the rock rolled into the water with a huge splash sending ripples all the way out across the lake. Then it was as though a geyser erupted from beneath the back end of Kyle's Dodge, but it didn't look like water that erupted from the ground.

The rear end of Kyle's car shot into the air, flipping the car over as it did a forward somersault into the lake with Kyle still sitting helplessly in the driver's seat. The boulder that had rolled in before it crumpled the roof as the car landed on top of it, but also kept the car mostly above the water at the shallow shore. Kyle was already scampering out the window, staring at the blood, red geyser as it continued to shoot up into the sky like Old Faithful for five more seconds and then it stopped as quickly as it had started. There was no red mess, in the water or on the ground. The only evidence that anything at all had happened was Kyle's car sitting upside on the water's edge.

Kyle waded to the shore and cautiously peered into the hole where the rock had been planted for so many years. There was something down there. He pulled out a bundle about as big as a football, wrapped in some kind of animal hide, tied shut with hair that looked more human than animal. He broke off the hair tying it closed and unrolled the hide on the ground. Lisa had finally gotten brave enough to get out of her van and stood watching breathlessly by his side.

Inside the animal hide was a grotesque looking, crudely made doll. It reminded Kyle of a voodoo doll he'd seen in a movie he couldn't remember but its head was not human and it had no features on its face. It didn't look like the creature from his dreams, but it probably could have passed for a close relative.

"We need some matches," Kyle said to Lisa. "They burned only his body last time. This time I want to burn his spirit."

Lisa produced an emergency lighter she always kept in her mini-van glove compartment and handed it to Kyle. When he lit the doll's arm, he could swear he felt the creature's voice vibrating his bones in a blood curdling scream. He didn't hear anything except Lisa's nervous breathing over his shoulder, but he felt it, deep down inside at the core of his being as the doll rapidly turned to ash.

Lisa and Kyle, though not for lack of effort, never met each other again in the same lucid dream, but they never ran into the creature again, either. They each lived out their lives together, in both the real world and the dream world, just as Dorothy was supposed to have done upon her return from Oz, happily ever after.

Billy

Billy

The first one I saw was in the hospital when I was eleven.

I was the pitcher for our little league baseball team, The Minneapolis Mosquitoes. Billy Ruttman, my next-door neighbor and life-long best friend, was the catcher. We were a great team that year, Billy and me. We'd been tossing the ball back and forth in our back yards for as long as I could remember. Through the years, me being stronger and he being smarter, it didn't take too long before he traded in his fielding glove for a catcher's mitt. I had the stuff; the curve, the slider, and the fast ball. Billy would squat down in his back yard and flash a one, two, or three between his legs and then put his glove where he wanted me to hit it and I, throwing from my own back yard, rarely missed his spot. Neither one of us were very good at putting a bat on the ball, but when we were out on the field together, neither was the entire other team.

It was the last game of the season, in fact, the last game we ever played together, when I pitched a fast ball that came straight back at me even faster, hitting me in the side of the head and knocking me out cold. I didn't regain consciousness until later that evening at the hospital, my parents and Billy waiting patiently at my bedside for me to wake up. The doctor said I had suffered a mild concussion and had actually been in a coma, but thankfully, a very short lived one. He told me that my brain had bounced off my skull from the impact, was probably just a mild bruise, and that I could most likely go home the next morning. I was put in a room with three other boys about my age, all of us in the final recovery stages of our particular injuries, all planning on being sent home within the next day or two.

I couldn't sleep in the hospital. The room was too big. None of my familiar posters were on the walls. I couldn't hear my parents watching TV beyond the door. And the boy with the new cast on his leg in the bed to my right was snoring. I had no brothers or sisters so I wasn't used to sleeping in a room with other people. Sure, Billy and I had spent many a weekend night together having sleepovers at either his house or mine, but we never slept. We'd sit up all night telling each other ghost stories or jokes or talking about girls, whispering so that our parents couldn't hear us, smothering our laughter in our pillows, and finally falling asleep for a few hours as the sun started to chase away the darkness.

The light from the hospital hallway that seeped through the gaping crack between the door and the floor reflected off the white walls and white ceiling enough that the room was only dim instead of dark. I was wishing I had taken my Mom up on her offer to bring my Walkman for the night's stay, but I was sure I'd be leaving in the morning and at the time felt it more fuss than it was worth. I thought about turning on the TV to help pass the time, but didn't want to wake my roommates. I wasn't at all tired after having spent the afternoon and most of the evening in a semi-coma after getting my bell rung in the baseball game.

I decided I could mute the TV and just watch the pictures for a while. Maybe I could bore myself to sleep. I reached for the remote sitting on the white bedside table. That was when I saw it.

At first I thought there might be a fire somewhere close by and a nurse would be racing into the room any second to usher us to safety. Grayish purple smoke was seeping into the room from under the door. But as quickly as it started, it stopped, and a cloud about the size of a beach ball hovered in front of the door as though assessing the room it had just entered. Looking at it more intently, it didn't look like smoke at all. It appeared more like a cloudy mirage, swirling within itself, constantly in motion, while staying stationary at the same time. I slowly brought my arm back to my side and lay still, watching the vaporous form from the corner of my eye as it crept toward the first of the beds. Hovering over the first boy, it moved in close to his face as he slept. It stayed there for a few seconds and then moved on to the next bed. I was in the fourth bed, next to the window, trying to decide if I should push the red button on the doohickie connected to the bed to summon for the nurse. I didn't know what it might do if I moved, so I remained as still as I could and held my breath.

Again, the cloud hovered over the next bed's occupant for a few seconds, as if studying him, and slowly moved on to the third bed. It didn't seem to be doing anything. It floated inches above each boy's face and then moved on to the next one. When it started to leave the snoring boy's bed next to mine, I closed my eyes and silently prayed that it would leave me alone, too. It was nearing the end of August and the room was air conditioned, but I suddenly felt my face grow a few degrees colder and I knew the cloud thing was directly over me, observing me. I told myself I was being foolish, a silly scardy-cat. I didn't believe in the bogeyman and vaporous cloudy mists can't actually see anything. But then, they don't move with purpose either, as this one seemed to be doing.

Seconds that felt like minutes slowly crept by until I could stand it no longer. I opened my eyes, hoping that the cloud had moved on. It hadn't. In the center of the smoky cloud, I saw what appeared to be two eyes. They were just slits in the mist with a little red dot in each, and they were definitely focused on me. They shifted back and forth slightly in the constant motion of the purplish haze. It was like looking at the eyes in a Picasso painting, not quite aligned right, except these were alive.

The eyes blinked.

I screamed.

The eyes in the purple haze suddenly became as wide as my own as I cried out for the nurse, its look of surprise as great as mine had been. It quickly rose away from my face towards the ceiling. The hospital door flew open and a nurse ran in to see who had screamed. The other boys had been awakened and were now propped up on one elbow, groggily looking my direction. I looked up towards the ceiling where the oddity had retreated, but it was gone.

With all the boys looking at me, the nurse made her way straight to my bedside. "Are you okay?" she asked. "Did you have a nightmare?"

It was obvious that the nurse hadn't seen the cloudy form as she came in or it would have certainly drawn her attention. It wasn't the type of thing one sees every day and it had still been rising away from my face when she burst in. I didn't understand how she could *not* have seen it.

I didn't want to say that I had a nightmare in front of the other boys, even though I knew I'd probably never see any of them again. But there was no way I could tell her about the eyes of a floating mist that had hovered over each of our beds checking us out, either. That would be even worse than admitting to a nightmare. I picked the lesser of the two evils.

"I guess it was just a dream," I said, trying to sound braver than I felt. I even tried for a moment to convince myself that I had been dreaming and had awakened from my own scream.

But I knew better. It had not been a dream, or a nightmare. It had been real. I didn't sleep a wink that night in the hospital.

I didn't tell anyone about what I had seen, not even Billy, at least not at first. Having graduated from the sixth grade, I started middle school a couple of weeks later with new classes and teachers and friends to keep my mind busy. The memory of the cloudy mist thing became more like a bad dream with each passing day.

* * *

It was at a pep rally for the basketball team a month later when I was reminded that it had not been a dream. Billy was sitting next to me. We were on the top bleachers in the gymnasium watching the cheerleaders go through their rehearsed routine when I saw two of the cloud things drift out of a vent in the high ceiling.

"I think I'm going to ask out Debbie," Billy said, jabbing me in the side with his elbow and pointing to the bouncing girls on the basketball court below us. "She's the one on the end there. She sits next to me in my English class."

I didn't even hear him. My eyes were glued to the ceiling.

"Hey," Billy said, when I didn't respond. "What's with you? You look like you saw a ghost or something."

I pointed to the two purple clouds hovering over the center of the gym. One was the same size as the first one I had seen in the hospital. The other was no bigger than a basketball. "Do you see those?"

"See what?" Billy asked, trying to follow where I was pointing.

"Those purple things. Two of them. They just came through the vent up there."

"Nothing there, dude. All the action is down on the floor," Billy said.

I watched as the two cloudy forms separated, the smaller one traveling toward us while the larger one was moving toward the opposite set of bleachers across the gym.

"One's coming our way," I said, trying not to sound panicky.

"One what?" Billy replied, following my eyes and searching the ceiling.

Glancing around at the two hundred or so students packed in the gym, I saw that no one else was pointing up at the ceiling. There were no screams coming from squeamish girls. No one was racing toward the exits in a panic, which is exactly what I felt like doing. Apparently I was the only one that could see them.

"Nothing," I said quickly, but kept a careful eye on the one that was headed toward our side of the gym.

"She lives only a few blocks from us," Billy said.

"Who does?" I asked, as the cloud thing descended and began hovering right in front of the face of a boy a few rows in front of us.

"Debbie! Man, you are out of it. You okay?"

"Yeah, fine," I said, not sounding very convincing even to my own ears.

The purple cloud moved on to the next student, and the next, hovering in front of each of their faces for four or five seconds before moving on. I couldn't see the little eyes with the red pupils from where I was sitting, but I knew they were there, floating unevenly in the middle of the mist, studying each student as it hovered in front of them. When it advanced up a row instead of down, I stood up grabbing Billy's arm. "Let's get out of here."

"Hey, man! What's your problem?" Billy protested. "This is the best part. We can go after the cheerleaders are done."

"Now!" I said, no longer hiding the panic that I felt. The cloud-thing that was a few rows in front of us seemed to notice me as I stood up. It slowly began to glide our direction and I pulled Billy up out of his seat. "Let's go!"

Billy stood but didn't move. I wanted to run, but the bleachers were too crowded. There would be no quick escape. The cloud thing reached us a second later. I froze. Billy was still standing next to me, staring at me like I had lost my mind. I watched as the cloud thing hovered in front of Billy's face for a second or two and then it turned to face me. Remembering how the first one I had seen in the hospital reacted when it realized I could see it, I pretended to be watching the cheerleaders while it floated in front of my face. I could see right through it while trying to focus on the cheerleaders, but I could also still see those little red dots checking me out. My face felt a slight chill and my stomach did a couple of somersaults while I tried desperately to ignore its presence. Three seconds later, it moved to the boy seated on my other side, and then to the next, slowly making its way down the aisle, pausing in front of each student as it went.

"Alright, alright," Billy said, shaking his elbow free of my grip. "Let go of me. People will think we're fags or something. Let's go. But you better have a good explanation. Are you sick or something?"

While we walked home, I told Billy about my hospital experience. It sounded just as ludicrous as I had thought it would when hearing it out loud. Billy kept looking at me as we walked as though he thought I was crazy, but he didn't interrupt. Then I told him what had just happened in the gymnasium.

"And you think one was right in front of my face?" he asked, when I had finished. "I didn't see anything."

"Apparently I'm the only one that can see them," I said. "But, yeah, it was there. Didn't you feel your face get a little colder for a second?"

"No. I didn't notice anything. Just you acting like a pansy."

We walked the rest of the way home in silence. I knew Billy wanted to believe me. He was my best friend and we knew each other's deepest secrets and desires. We arrived at his driveway, mine being a few yards farther up the sidewalk, where we usually parted from our daily walk home to go inside our respective houses and put away our books and grab our mitts or a football to toss around in the backyard until called in for dinner, and he paused. Swiping a hand through his stringy brown hair getting it out of his eyes to see me better, he said, "Look, I don't know if what you think you saw was real or not, but I've never seen you scared before and right now you look terrible."

"It was real," I said. "I was beginning to doubt the first one was, but now I know for sure. They're real. I just don't know why I'm the only one that can see them."

"Just lucky, I guess," Billy said jokingly, trying to make me smile.

"Yeah, well this kind of luck I could do without." I said. "You gotta believe me, man. I'm not going crazy."

"I believe you, I guess. But I also think you're crazy." Billy said with a smile, and a playful jab at my shoulder. "Go put your stuff away. I'll meet you out back."

I went up my own driveway and into the empty house, my parents not home from work yet, and threw my books on my bed. I wasn't up for catch. I was still feeling a bit shaken from the second sighting, but I was glad I had told Billy about them. It made me feel less alone even though I was apparently the only one that could see them. I left the mitt and balls where they lay and headed out to the backyard with my head down and my hands stuffed in the pockets of my jeans. Billy joined me a few minutes later carrying his backpack with him.

"Tree house," he said.

It wasn't really a tree house. There was a big oak tree that separated our yards. A rope ladder hung down from its lowest branch about fifteen feet up, leading to a heavy flat board that we laid over the branches and nailed a few supports to. It was only about seven feet across the board in any direction, but provided plenty of room for a couple of kids to move around on and plenty of privacy for us to share our secrets. I followed Billy up the ladder.

"I brought a couple of my Dad's books," Billy said, after I pulled myself up over the edge and sat down next to him. "He's always been into weird stuff. Wizards, witches, demons, old myths; things like that."

"I never thought your Dad was weird," I said.

"He's not," Billy laughed. "He just thinks a lot of the things people have believed in are fascinating. It's not like he believes in them. I think he uses them for ideas when he's writing. I like to look at the pictures. There're some really cool looking ghouls and demons in these two. I wanted to see if you thought any of them looked like what you saw."

I immediately started leafing through the books but I couldn't find anything even close to what I had seen. We did find a lot of things that looked a lot scarier than the purple clouds with eyes, and a lot more dangerous, too. But just as we were closing up the second of the books, Billy's Mom stuck her head out the back door and hollered for Billy to come in and wash up for dinner.

"Has your Dad got any more of these?" I asked him, as he put the books back into his backpack.

"Yeah. He's got a ton of them. Maybe you can sleepover this weekend and we can look at more."

"I'll ask my Mom," I told him, and we climbed down the ladder to go join our families for dinner.

My Mom said it was fine if I spent the night with Billy that Friday night and we looked through a ton more of his Dad's books all night long, freaking ourselves out with mythical grotesquities of the past, but we didn't see anything that looked like what I had described. Nor did I encounter any more purple clouds hovering in front of anyone's face over the next three years. Billy and I brought up the subject less and less frequently and before long, it was no more than an inside joke, though Billy always thought the joke a bit funnier than I did.

* * *

The summer before we were changing schools again, about to become freshmen in high school, Billy and Debbie and Janice and I were out swimming in the lake a few blocks from our homes when something happened that brought the subject to mind once again. Billy and Debbie had been holding hands in the hallways between classes for almost two years and I was trying to work up the courage to ask Janice if she'd be my steady.

The four of us were in the middle of the small lake sitting on the wooden float that gives rest for those strong enough to swim out to it. Billy and Debbie were chatting away while Janice and I shyly looked anywhere but at each other, me wondering if I could ask, she wondering when I would ask. I was never as smooth with the girls as Billy was. Billy gave Debbie a wink and nodded towards Janice and me with a devilish smile, indicating that they should give us some space, both already fully aware of my intention to ask out Janice, and the two of them dove off the platform and began racing each other to the shore. Both were strong swimmers.

A few silent, uncomfortable minutes passed while I summoned my courage. Just as we both started to speak at once, we heard Billy yelling at us. I turned and saw him standing alone on the beach, running back and forth along the water's edge.

"Where is she?!" he screamed. "You see her?!"

Then he dove back into the water and I knew instantly there was trouble. Janice and I both dove in too, swimming as fast as we could towards Billy. We all met in the middle where Debbie was floating face down. Billy got her turned over and we saw a gash on her forehead leaking blood. She was unconscious as the three of us got her to shore and laid her on the beach. Billy put his head on her chest.

"She isn't breathing," he said. "I think she went too low and hit her head on a rock or something."

Billy was smart, quick to act, and always ready to take control. He was a natural leader and never panicked.

"Sean, go get my bandana by my towel," he said to me, in a steadier voice than I could have mustered at that point. "Tie it around her head to stop the bleeding. Janice, go find a house with someone home and call an ambulance."

"Is she going to be alright?" Janice asked, tears welling up in her eyes.

"Maybe. Just go! Hurry!"

I returned with the bandana and Billy was already administering CPR like he'd done it a hundred times before, pushing twice on her chest, then putting his mouth over hers while holding her nose shut and forcing air into her lungs, then starting over again. I was tying the bandana around her head when it happened. A little yellowish pink cloud the size of a baseball appeared to leak out of her eyes. I jumped back.

"Tie it tighter," Billy said when he saw me jump back. "You need to stop the bleeding!"

"Did you see that?" I asked. It had looked just like the purple clouds except it was smaller and much brighter.

"See what?! I'm trying to get her breathing again," he yelled at me. "She's swallowed a lot of water. Get over here!"

"I'm on it," I said, pushing aside the memories of the purple clouds that had just come flooding back.

"Still not breathing," Billy said. He put a hand to her neck. "I can't feel a pulse."

I thought he was going to give up, but then he pounded on her chest hard once, twice, and I was about to ask him what the hell he thought he was doing to her when she suddenly coughed up some water and started to breathe again while still struggling to cough up a little more of the lake. She moaned and Billy turned her on her side and more lake water spilled out of her mouth.

Just then, Janice was running back to the beach with two adults and announced that an ambulance should be arriving in less than five minutes. The paramedics arrived even a minute faster than that and we had to step back getting out their way. The adults from the house whose phone Janice had used gave us a ride to the hospital. When we arrived, Debbie had already been taken to a doctor and the paramedics were walking out the emergency entrance.

"So who applied the CPR?" one of them asked as he saw the three of us approaching.

"He did," I offered, pointing to Billy.

"Well," he said, walking toward Billy with his hand out, "I'd like to shake your hand. I think you saved her life. It's good to know that there are young folk out there like yourself that know what to do in a crisis. I've seen too many that don't. She wouldn't have stood a chance if you three had waited for us to arrive."

"She's going to be alright, then?" Billy asked.

"You'll have to ask the doctor, but I'd guess yes," the paramedic said, and then adding with a smile, "Thanks to you."

We went into the hospital and found where she had been taken and waited for the doctor to come out. A half an hour later, he finally did.

"She took a nasty bump on the head and is having a little trouble remaining conscious right now," the doctor informed us. Then he smiled. "But I think she is going to be fine."

The doctor then also praised Billy for his quick responsiveness, repeating how he had saved her life with his CPR knowledge and quick actions. I had almost forgotten about the little yellow-pink cloud in all the bustle and worry. But since Debbie was apparently going to be okay, I decided not to mention it to the doctor. I didn't think he'd have any answers for me if I did, anyway.

As it turned out, she wasn't alright. For a while, everyone blamed it on depression, having a near death experience, or some other psychological mumbo jumbo. She seemed to have no joy left in her. She didn't leave the house after getting out of the hospital until school started. Once in school, she was never the bubbly, light-hearted person that she had been before. She had been a straight-A student before the accident, now her work was just passable, nothing that reflected much thought or care. It was as though she was just regurgitating information. She more closely resembled a living robot, going through all the motions, smiling only when others smiled, responding only to questions, never contributing with a thought of her own. She quit hanging around with all her friends and never looked for Billy between classes. He always had to go find her.

One afternoon when we were walking home after school, I asked him if he thought she had changed.

"Well, yeah," he said gloomily. "She doesn't seem to care about anything anymore."

"Is she sad because she almost died?" I asked.

"That's what's weird about it," he said. He stopped walking and turned to face me. "She doesn't seem sad, but she doesn't seem happy about anything, either. She used to be very emotional. She always spoke her mind. It was one of the things I liked about her. It was who she was. Now it's like she doesn't even have any thoughts. I can't explain it really. It's like she's lost her personality"

"She hasn't told you anything about why she's been so withdrawn?"

"Not a word," Billy replied. "I mean, I figured I'd earned a few brownie points and maybe even free passage to second base by saving her life and all, but she won't even talk anymore. But it's not like she tells me to go away or anything.

She doesn't act mad at me. She let me kiss her once, but it was like kissing my sister or something. No feelings. She just sat there. And her eyes don't shine anymore. I used to love her eyes." He paused, thought for a second, and then added, "I asked her if she still liked me and she said, '*sure, why not*', like I had just asked her if she wanted a pop or something. It's like she doesn't even care. I don't know what's up with her, but I'm about to ask her if she wants to split up. And the way she's been acting, I expect her answer will be, '*sure, why not.*'"

Later that evening, in the tree house, I told Billy about the pink cloud I saw slip out through her eyes.

"What do you think it was?" I asked him.

"I don't know," he answered. "But it doesn't sound good."

Debbie's reply when he broke up with her a week later was very close to his prediction. He told me that he was going to do it when we were on the way to school that morning and said he felt really bad about it, but he was giving up trying to find the spark in her that had apparently been extinguished due to the accident. But I think he felt even worse when she simply responded "Okay," and then walked off to class as though it had made no difference to her either way.

A month later, the trouble began. Billy told me that she refused to take a test in their math class and started swearing at the teacher. Then she started throwing everything she could get her hands on at him. It took the math instructor and the science instructor to physically restrain her and haul her down to the principal's office. She didn't come back to school. No one I knew ever saw her again. A year later, we heard that she killed both her parents before turning her Dad's gun on herself. I didn't believe it, thought it was just the high school rumor mill drumming up some drama, but that evening, it was headline news on every TV channel.

"What do you think happened to her?" Billy asked me the next day. He wasn't expecting an answer, but I had thought about it a lot too, and had one for him anyway.

"I think she died at the lake, Billy. I think that pink thing I saw come out of her eyes while you were giving her the CPR was her life force or something. Then you brought her heart back to life, but that was after she had already lost something important."

"What, like her soul or something going off to Heaven?" he asked sarcastically, not giving my thought much credence.

"Yeah," I said, unable to meet his eyes. "Something like that."

"But what made her go crazy all of a sudden a couple of months later," he asked.

I didn't have an answer for that one.

He continued, talking to himself as much as to me. "I mean, she killed her parents, for God's sake. I knew her. She would never have done something like that. She once told me she had the best parents in the world. But that was before the accident. Afterwards, I guess nobody knew what she was thinking, but she didn't seem to care enough about anyone in the first place anymore. Certainly not enough to actually kill them."

"At least not until that time she went berserk in class," I reminded him.

"Yeah, that was really weird. So what the hell happened? What made her crack?"

Billy had been that way as long as I had known him, since we were little kids. He always had to know the answers. That's why he was so smart. He hated not knowing the answers.

For a while, Billy couldn't let it go. He started reading books about different psychoses and forms of insanity. He was determined to try to figure out what had happened to

Debbie, almost obsessive about it. Being his best friend, I was the one he bounced his ideas off of.

"I was reading about serial killers," he said to me one day while we were hanging out in my backyard. We didn't use the tree house anymore. We were too big and heavy for the board that served as the platform. "Look at this list I made." He handed me a piece of notebook paper on which he had compiled a list of about twenty names, each accompanied by two dates. I recognized a couple of names, but not many.

"So what are the dates for?" I asked.

"The first date is the date of their first known killing," he explained. "The second date, which is always earlier than the first one, represents some near-death experience or major injury that they had."

"Just like Debbie,"

"Yeah," he nodded. "Just like Debbie." Then he asked, "You ever seen any more of those purple cloud things you saw at the gym that time?"

"No, I haven't. Why? What are you thinking?"

He pulled out an old looking book. "I found this at the library yesterday," he said, opening it to a page he had previously set a bookmarker in. "The county library, not the school one. It talks about the soul and how the eyes are 'the windows to the soul'. It reminded me of when you told me a few days ago about seeing something cloud-like leak out of Debbie's eyes while she wasn't breathing. I think you were right. She had died and I brought her back, but I was too late."

"That would explain her initial change," I said. "But it doesn't explain why she suddenly cracked a couple of months later, or why she killed her parents and herself after that."

"I know," Billy said, "but this might." He opened the other book he had brought outside with him, also bookmarked.

"This book describes old American Indian rituals and beliefs. One of the shorter chapters is about the *Demon's Eye*. They say that the *Demon's Eye* can't be seen by the human eye but that it travels the world looking for people that have lost their soul and then it moves in and lives in the place that the soul had left vacant. They say it is pure evil. They would try to destroy the demon by gouging out the eyes of the person that it had inhabited."

I was beginning to see where he was going with this. The pieces were beginning to fit together. "You think the pink cloud I saw was her soul escaping through the eyes and the purple ones were the *Demon's Eye* that book talks about and they got into Debbie?"

"Yeah, that's exactly what I think. But no one can describe the *Demon's Eye* because no one has ever seen them. Except you."

"Why me?" I asked, not expecting an answer.

"Brain damage. The first time you saw one was after getting your brain knocked around. And you saw them in a hospital," he added. "What better place to find a person who had died and been resurrected."

"So why did it take two months before Debbie was infected? She'd been in the hospital for a week after the accident."

"Maybe there aren't many of them around. Maybe they are always traveling around looking for soulless people but don't stay in one place and stake it out. I don't know. But you see them and you've only seen three of them in more than three years so I'm guessing there aren't a whole lot of them out there." Then he looked me right in the eye and said, "I'm serious Sean, if I ever lose my soul, don't gouge my eyes out, just kill me."

"I hear you," I said. "Same goes for me. I don't want to become a serial killer."

We each held up our right hand and our pinky fingers wrapped together and pumped once. It was a pact.

* * *

Time is the most natural and efficient of healers. Time allowed Billy to forget about Debbie and move on. Time, and avoiding hospitals and large gatherings of people as best I could, allowed me to forget about pink and purple clouds and uneven eyes with red pupils. He had several girlfriends during the remainder of our high school days. I had a couple. We both applied to, and were accepted by, the University of Minnesota. He was studying English, already working on his first novel, wanting to be a fiction writer like his Dad. I was a business major. We were roommates our freshman year, still and forever the best of friends.

Then it happened.

We had just left our favorite diner in Dinky Town, the university's shopping and dining area, when a drunk driver hit a car in the street. The car it hit veered of the road trying unsuccessfully to avoid the collision and struck both of us. I had only been grazed by the side of the car, breaking my leg and my hip. Billy had been a few feet closer to the street, directly in the car's path. As we lay there on the sidewalk side by side, I turned my head to look for Billy just in time to see a small pink cloud exit through his open, but expressionless eyes. The last thing I remembered before passing out was hoping that my friend had died.

Billy was in surgery all night. By morning, his doctor told me that he was in serious, but stable condition. I asked if I could see him but had to wait three days before I was allowed to talk to him. I wheeled myself to his room. He was in one of those observation rooms with the glass wall. He was just lying there, staring at the ceiling. He was awake, but didn't respond to me when I asked how he was doing. I snapped my fingers in front of his face to get his attention and he slowly moved his head my direction, finally acknowledging my presence, by with no recognition in his lifeless eyes. He just stared at me, emotionlessly. I asked again how he was doing and he replied with a shrug of the shoulders and returned his gaze to the ceiling.

Later that afternoon, I tried again. He was awake, still staring at the ceiling. I asked him how he was doing and he spoke a single word without even looking my direction.

"Okay".

"Billy," I said, "it's me, Sean. You're going to be fine".

"Okay," he replied again, still looking at the ceiling.

I followed his gaze to the ceiling and saw it hovering there. The purple cloud with the little red dots floating in its center. I didn't think Billy could see it because the expression on his face remained unchanged as the cloud began to descend and came to a stop inches in front of his face. Instinctively, as I would have done had I seen a snake or a rat approaching my friend's face while he slept, even though he was awake at this time, I shouted "Hey!" at the purple mist, but only half-heartedly swatted at it, not wanting to touch it or actually sink my hand into its swirling vapors. I wonder still today if maybe I had sunk my hand into the cloud rattling those tiny red eyes, if things would have turned out differently. But it might have just delayed the inevitable. Billy's soul, or whatever the pink cloud was supposed to be, had long since departed leaving only the husk of the friend I had once known.

The purple mist quickly shifted its gaze to me, its beady red eyes locking on to mine for a brief second, looking as shocked as I was that I could see it, before it turned immediately back to Billy.

I watched in horror as the purple mist seemed to get absorbed by Billy's eyes. A mere second later, the cloud was gone.

I didn't go into see Billy the next morning. I was released with crutches the following day. I went to the pawn shop and had to wait three more days but finally my background check was approved and the owner gave me the gun I had purchased.

I went back to the hospital and walked straight into Billy's room. He turned and looked at me, anger on his face, hatred in his eyes, looking not like the friend I had known my entire life, but more like a stranger that wanted to hurt something, or someone. I noticed his arms had been tied down to his sides and restrained by the nurse or the doctor, obviously believing he was a threat to harm himself or others. He hurled a few obscenities my direction and yelled at me to get the hell out. Without hesitation or saying a single word, through my tears, I shot him in the chest.

*　*　*

I tried to explain to the jury that I hadn't killed Billy; that he had died in the accident. I told them that I was doing for him exactly what I would have hoped that he would have done for me; that I had only done something that he had asked me to do several years earlier; that we had a pact; that it was what Billy wanted. My lawyer tried to cop an insanity plea when I told the jury and judge about the soul I saw leaving him at the scene of the accident and then about the *Demon's Eye* I saw enter him in the hospital. The trial was put on hold while I went through a psychological evaluation. I was deemed sane, as I knew I would be because I am indeed quite sane. The jury said I knew what I was doing. They were right about that, of course, but I had never really expected them to believe or condone my motivation.

Billy was my best friend. He was a good man. He will always be remembered fondly by those that had known him. I know that killing him was the best way I could thank him for the great friendship we had shared.

I asked for the death penalty, but got forty years instead. It turns out one really can get anything one desires in prison if you have the money. Apparently, the guards don't make enough. One of the guards was more than happy to supply me with a knife for the right price. He didn't even ask who I was going to use it on. I am hoping when my soul begins its journey later today and escapes through my eyes, that it will find Billy waiting for me. I can't wait to see him again. He's my best friend…forever and always.

Cloud Nine

Cloud Nine

Ted's last thoughts were not the panicky, desperate thoughts he would have guessed they'd have been had anyone ever asked, but no one ever had and he found himself strangely calm as the earth grew closer by the second. There was of course that brief first moment of terror, that moment of realization that today simply wasn't going to end the way you had planned; that moment when you scream, "Shit!" and hope that by saying it, you won't do it.

Then there was denial. "This isn't actually happening. I'll wake up any second now."

But Ted knew better. He'd been on his way to a conference in Seattle. It was a relatively short flight from San Francisco and he knew he hadn't fallen asleep. The hijacking, the deafening gun shots inside the small plane, the wind rushing against his face; this was no nightmare. This was the real McCoy.

He was not an angry soul, had always accepted things for what they are. He felt no anger towards his situation or to those who had put him in it. The world was what it was. Living in it was the risk we all take. The situation is what it is. If he could do it over again, he couldn't imagine doing it any other way. So the anger stage was skipped altogether.

He was not a religious man so he had no God to pray to, to ask for help. He didn't believe in miracles. Everything is what it is.

He had a pretty good idea what the result of his action was going to be before he went through with it. And even though he made up his mind to act in a split-second, that was all the time he needed to know that it was the right thing to do and was worth the potential price. The hijacker had already killed two people, one of whom had undoubtedly come to the same decision but whose opportunity had vanished too quickly. Maybe he hadn't noticed it in time. Maybe he took a second too long weighing the risk. But the hijacker had turned already pulling the trigger and a hero lay bleeding in the aisle.

The hijacker dragged the dying man by a leg with one arm towards the front of the plane, swinging his rapid-fire pistol from side to side with the other, already having displayed his willingness to shoot anyone who moved. No one did. He only had to drag him a few feet to the exit hatch. The plane was small, no first class section. It was at full passenger capacity, however, thirty-two in all. Ted was in row A, the aisle seat.

The whole event took no more than sixty seconds and it was this that was running through Ted's mind as the wind sped past his ears, pulling his lips tight against his face. He was falling spread-eagled to slow the fall, as he had seen sky-divers do on TV, not so much to delay his inevitable death by a few precious seconds, but to lessen the roar of the wind in his ears. Yet as he replayed those last sixty seconds in his mind a couple of times, knowing he had only another sixty or so left to live, he managed a strained smile against the pounding wind and couldn't help but take note of his lack of panic.

Ten minutes after the plane had taken off from San Francisco International, the hijacker had stood up from his seat one row back and across the aisle from Ted. He quickly announced his intentions to take the plane to Mexico and showed off his gun, threatening to shoot anyone who moved. The locked door to the cockpit had opened, the co-pilot having decided (unwisely and against regulations) to see what all the commotion was about. The hijacker turned and shot him in the forehead just above his disbelieving eyes as though it had been part of the plan and started screaming orders to the pilot to turn the plane around and aim for Mexico. The man in the seat behind Ted, a young twenty-something with long blond hair tied neatly in a ponytail stretching half-way down his back, stood and charged the moment the hijacker turned his body. He must have hoped the element of surprise would be enough, but the gunman heard him coming and turned around firing. The charging man was halted in his tracks and thrown backwards as a trio of bullets opened his chest, adding new streaks of red to his green and yellow tie-dyed t-shirt.

Waving his gun wildly at the terrified passengers, the hijacker moved to the plane's hatch and began struggling with its handle. The sole stewardess aboard had been aiding a passenger near the rear of the plane when the hijacker had first risen from his seat; now realizing the madman's intentions, she screamed "You can't open that!", but was too late. Ted knew he was the only one that would have the opportunity. Two wide-eyed, scared children were seated in row A opposite himself, a small divider between themselves and the hatch. He was the only one who might be able to reach the hijacker and the hatch quickly enough to avoid being shot. There had been only a split-second of time available to react and it was during that instant that Ted had seen his opportunity, weighed the consequences, and taken action.

The young man was surely a fallen hero. Without his attempt to overtake the hijacker, Ted's opportunity would not have arisen and who knows how many more might have died at the hand of the trigger-happy madman. And he himself was also a hero, he told himself. Although his ego had no need to be flattered, he still granted himself another smile in death's face at the thought. He was going to die a hero. Who'd of thunk it?

Maybe the fact that he knew what he was doing when he did it is why he felt no panic, no remorse, no fear. He was only thirty-eight years old. He had plenty of years ahead of him under any other circumstance, but he felt he had lived a good life and he knew he had done the right thing. His wife and sixteen year old son would of course be devastated, but he had good insurance. They would be taken care of. His son would certainly understand why his father had done what he did and pride would soon overcome the despair and anguish of the loss. His wife was still young enough to find true love again.

Reflection, he thought. How typical. He calmly tried to think of something else. Reflection might cause remorse and he didn't want remorse tainting his moment as a hero. But death seemed to be the subject of the moment, hero or no hero, and it was hard to take his mind from it. His thoughts drifted quickly to how he was going to die, free-falling from an airplane without a parachute, and he began comparing this to other ways that he might have died. Fire, drowning, cancer, heart attack, disease, gun shot from a hijacker…all of which required a duration of pain, some not so long, some lasting for years. Ted felt no pain, doubted he would even have time to feel any pain between his sudden impact with Mother Earth and that moment when his brain would shut down and all feeling would cease. And even if he did feel the collision, how long could it last? He decided he wouldn't be alive long enough for his brain to even register the pain once he landed and therefore concluded that if one had to choose a way to go, this would be his choice. So how could he complain?

But he hadn't chosen to die, just as he hadn't chosen to be heroic. He simply reacted to an emergency situation. Calmly, sanely, quickly, he chose to do what he thought was best for all. Paying no attention to the stewardess' warning, the hijacker had thrown open the hatch to dispose of the blond man's bleeding body. Chaos briefly filled the small plane as the hero's body and any and all loose items in the plane were immediately sucked through the doorway and into the great beyond. A man a couple of rows back yelled, "He's going to kill us all!" and the initial shock of the event was transformed into screaming and panic from most of the passengers. The hijacker was also briefly in a state of alarm and confusion as he grabbed for the luggage rack above the doorway barely in time to keep himself from being swept out into the sky as the plane trembled and shuddered violently with the sudden change in air pressure. Ted chose to rush the hijacker before he could get the hatch shut. Of course, ideally he had hoped to push the hijacker out, somehow get the hatch closed, and be done with it. His greatest fear in that split second while turning thought into action was of getting shot by the hijacker before he got to him. But he calculated that even if he was shot, with the small amount of space to be covered, his initial momentum would allow him success in trying to dispatch the hijacker from the plane. Also still in that instant of a second, he realized that same momentum, if he was not shot, might cause him to fly out of the plane with the hijacker.

And that was the way it went down. The hijacker had seen him coming but this time surprise had worked in favor of the home team. The hijacker's hand on the luggage rack came free as he grabbed for Ted who was on him almost as fast as he had gotten up from his seat. Only sixty seconds after the madman had risen from his own seat and killed two people.

Ted and the hijacker had followed the dying blond man out of the plane into the sky, still locked together in a bear hug, looking like lovers seeking solace and comfort from each other as they tumbled head over heels into the high summer air. The hijacker pushed himself away and even triggered off a couple of rounds aimed at Ted but the shots sprayed harmlessly as he started spiraling away towards earth. Ted calmly spread out his arms and legs like he'd seen the skydivers do and watched the hijacker turn a few cartwheels while screaming bloody murder and squeezing off a few more aimless rounds. Looking over his shoulder back up at the small plane, he saw the hatch of the plane draw closed. Despite the fact that he was on the wrong side of the door soaring to his death, he found himself pleased with the result of his actions, sure that he had done the right thing even in the face of the consequences. Already some fifty yards closer to the earth in his out of control somersault, Ted watched the madman turn the gun on himself and make his final kill. The cartwheel sped up with its dead weight, the flying limbs became a blur, and Ted erased the man and the image from his mind. He had more important things to think about in his final minute.

The view, for example, was one few people will ever see. Puffy white clouds were scattered about looking like huge cotton pillows shading large sections of the earth below. The sun felt warm and comforting on his back. The consistent drone of the wind had become soothing like a familiar mantra. Truly there was no better way to die than falling from a plane.

Remembering the skydiving program he had seen on TV, he tried to aim for the largest of the clouds still below him and a little off to the right. Ted dipped his right arm, shoulder, and head towards the cloud, imagining he was Superman with his cape flailing in the air. Another experience few people would get the opportunity to enjoy, flying through a cloud like a bird, like Superman, actually feeling the moisture as it slowly gathers in anticipation of becoming rain. The thought excited him and he dipped his head a little more, speeding up his descent towards the cloud.

As he entered the massive cloud three seconds later, the temperature noticeably dropped and chilled his skin. His vision was suddenly limited and his depth perception could not be trusted inside the dense, puffy, white mist. He found it impossible to determine if he was seeing inches, feet, or even miles in front of him. As he fought the force of the onrushing wind to wipe the moisture from his brow, he thought he caught movement from his left, just on the edge of his peripheral vision, turned his head that direction, and saw nothing. He hoped a plane wouldn't be passing through the cloud at that particular moment. That wasn't part of the deal here. He had already accepted his means of demise and had no desire to be splattered on a windshield like a bug on the highway. Even if the plane only grazed him, it would definitely be painful, he decided, and the rest of this wondrous last flight would be ruined.

Seconds passed and he was still immersed in the wet, white oasis of the sky, but the wind in his ears had quieted a bit. The sun no longer warmed his back and the whiteness had turned to a dull gray. He felt exhilarated, even privileged, to be allowed to spend a few of his final seconds viewing firsthand what most people could only dream about. His only regret was the realization that he would be exiting the cloud before he had time to explore it.

More seconds passed. He was still in the cloud, and once again he was sure he caught movement on his left, turned his head, and saw nothing but more gray cloud. Shouldn't he be exiting the cloud by now, he thought? He was no expert; he had no idea how deep clouds actually were from his life of casual observation from the ground. He had no idea how fast one travels through the air when free-falling from a plane and he could only guess at the number of seconds it would take to impact the earth. But he had been in this cloud for, what, ten seconds now? Fifteen? Or maybe it was only two or three and his own mind had slowed time for him so that he could better enjoy his final descent. He knew the mind did some pretty amazing stuff when under stress. But he felt no stress. He had immediately accepted his situation for what it was.

But still, the cloud continued.

Maybe, he reasoned, he had hit a cloud that extended all the way to the ground. Maybe this cloud was a ground level fog. He may not even see the ground coming. He wouldn't even know when he was going to hit the earth. He wouldn't even know he was dead.

Maybe that was it, he thought, still soaring through the cloud. He was already dead. He had splattered into the earth and his brain hadn't been able to register the impact so it clung to its last memory, the cloud, and would forever be replaying that final memory with no new stimuli ever capable of intervening.

That had to be it. He was going on half a minute now encased in the moist, chilled cloud. One didn't have to be a scientist or a physicist to know this was not right. Even if the cloud did lay on the earth as a large, bothersome fog bank, he felt he should have reached his destination by now and he thought it ironic that his first worry since exiting the plane with the hijacker was that he *wasn't* dead yet. He had heard somewhere that most people, when free-falling from a plane without a parachute, die of a heart-attack before ever reaching the earth. He knew he had not had a heart-attack. He could feel his heart beating in his chest, certainly a little harder and faster than normal, but it was definitely still beating.

And still the fall, the cloud, the heartbeat, continued.

Ted slid his tongue between his teeth and bit down, letting up on the bite immediately when his tongue complained of the pain. No, he was definitely not dead yet. He could still feel pain. His heart was still beating. And the wind still roared in his ears. Roared? Not exactly the roar it had been when he had approached the cloud. Now it was more like riding a motorcycle into the wind without a helmet. Apparently clouds blocked out more than just the sun. The atmosphere within seemed a little thinner, as well. Just as many animals can change their color or even their shape to protect themselves from predators, maybe a cloud somehow protects itself from the wind.

Another five, ten, fifteen seconds passed. Another movement, this time to his right. Glancing that way he thought he saw a face but it was gone the moment he focused in that direction. He remembered how when young, he and his little brother would lay in the grass in the backyard looking up at the clouds announcing all the shapes they saw them form. A boat, a hand, a duck. They'd watch as a cloud-horse would morph into a cloud-castle complete with a little cloud-moat floating at its base and "ooohh" and "aaahh" as they noticed what the other had pointed out. On a few occasions, Ted claimed to see faces in the cloud formations, watching down on them as they watched up. He thought that would be cool and he imagined a couple of cloud-people, brothers like he and Greg, lying up there on their cloud-pillow, gazing down at the earth, naming the shapes they saw passing beneath them. Little Greg thought that was creepy, but he also still believed in the bogeyman. Ted, being the caring and understanding big brother that he was even at the age of seven, would then always renounce his discovery and claim, "It's gone. Now it looks like a duck." But that wasn't always the case. Sometimes the faces lingered. Sometimes while other clouds were constantly morphing in and out of new shapes, Ted thought the faces continued to watch.

Wiping the condensation from his brow again, using noticeably less effort against the wind, Ted definitely saw movement this time. It was below him, slightly off to the left but directly in his line of vision. The clouds, it seemed, formed as many shapes on the inside as they appeared to on the outside when gazing up at them from the ground. But from here, their shapes were formed with shades of white on gray instead of using the blue sky as its canvas. What first appeared to be swirling little mists of gray cloud formed a perfect circle with a defined edge in its different shades of gray and white. The circle stretched into an oval and four more circles appeared within the first. The oval was expanding, or Ted was simply getting closer causing it to appear to grow in size, he wasn't sure which, but the smaller circles in their own shades of gray also began to take individual form. Ted watched in fascination, almost forgetting that he was in the process of plummeting to his death, as the cloudy forms within the cloud took on the shape of a face. The eyes of the cloud-face appeared to be looking at him, studying him with the same fascination that he was studying it. A puffy off-white beard formed at its chin giving the face an aged look. It reminded Ted of a stone carving of Zeus he had seen when studying Greek mythology in college.

Movement again to his right distracted his attention from the cloud-carving of Zeus. Snapping his head in that direction, what looked like a giant hand appeared to be coming at him. It looked as though it were half a clap and Ted thought if he looked the other direction he would see the other half of the clap closing in on him, the two hands preparing to squash him like a bothersome gnat hovering over one's food at a picnic in the park. The wind suddenly seemed to shift miraculously, coming at him from the right where the approaching hand was as much as it was coming up at him from the ground. It felt like a gentle push.

The feeling of being pushed vanished as quickly as it had started and the hand appeared to dissipate back into random slices of swirling gray mist. Returning his gaze below, thinking that any second the earth would appear and he could begin the countdown to his contact with the ground, hoping he would not land in a busy mall parking lot or the infield of a little league baseball game in progress, he noticed that the gentle push the cloud-hand had given him aligned him directly above the cloud-carving of Zeus. The face had grown large without losing its shape, as large as a small house. The eyes had grown so distinct and intense that they almost looked intelligent. The mouth was now agape and beyond its gray lips appeared to be blackness darker than the darkest storm cloud he had ever seen.

Instinctively, Ted dipped his left shoulder and arm, not wanting to fall through the mouth and into the blackness, but the face seemed to stay with him, directly in his path. Two seconds later, Ted was swallowed by the blackness.

* * *

Ted's mind woke up before his eyes did. His eyes still felt glued shut by the Sandman and he couldn't immediately open them. Suddenly he remembered that he had never expected to be opening them again in the first place. He remembered the plane, the hijacker, and flying through the air like Superman. He remembered the gunman cartwheeling through the air before him after turning his gun on himself, and he remembered entering the cloud. After that, he wasn't sure. He vaguely remembered being surprised by seeing shapes form inside the cloud much like they do when observed from the ground, and the feeling of being watched, but that was where his memory got a little foggy. He should be dead. That much he was sure of. The idea that he was thinking about trying to open his eyes, that he was consciously thinking about anything at all, just didn't make any sense. Dead men don't think, he thought.

Using all his willpower against the Sandman, he tried again to force his eyes open and for the briefest moment succeeded, but the brightness forced them shut again before he could register anything but white. He had died, he decided. He must be in Heaven. Of course, he had never believed in Heaven but it seemed the only answer. People simply don't wake up after free-falling from a plane without a parachute.

And what was he lying on? He felt nothing, not a soft mattress, not even the hard ground or a floor. He assumed he was lying down but only because he was just gaining consciousness like one does when waking from a long sleep. His arms and legs felt slightly stiff but movable and he moved one of his arms to determine what his bed was made of. He felt nothing.

Some wind tousled his hair and chilled his skin. He was outside, he thought. Wanting desperately to open his eyes, to assess his current situation, he brought both stiff arms to his face and shielded his closed eyes like a child counting to twenty in a game of Hide and Seek before trying to open them again against the brightness that had instantly slammed them shut on his first attempt. His fingers glowed with a red outline from the brightness that lay behind them, but at least his eyes were now open. Slowly, little by little, he spread his fingers enough to let in some of the light. It stung his eyes but they remained open this time as the pupils slowly adjusted to the brightness. Still all Ted could see, however, was slits of whiteness behind his glowing fingers.

The hospital, Ted thought. They were always a sanitary white. White walls, white ceilings, white sheets, white light. Maybe he was suspended in the air after breaking every bone in his body from the fall. But that would mean he had survived his fall and he didn't understand how that could be possible. Yet here he was, thinking, a little sore (but not the type of sore one would expect after breaking every bone in one's body), holding his hands in front of his face. He certainly felt alive despite its impossibility.

Two long minutes passed before he was able to completely remove his hands from his face to confirm what his racing mind thought he was seeing from between the gaps of his fingers. Swirling mists of cloud. He was still alive, had not gone crashing into the earth but had been *caught* somehow by the cloud itself. Below, above, to the right, and to the left, all he could see was gray and white swirling cloud. He felt like he was standing up, too, not lying down as he had first assumed, yet he felt no floor beneath his feet. He must be dreaming, he thought. But he knew he wasn't dreaming. It was merely the only explanation his mind could generate.

Before him, the mist seemed to be moving as though with purpose. A moment later he was peering at what looked like a pencil sketching of a cloud-staircase. The steps were white, the risers in shades of gray. At the top of the stairs appeared another face, not as large as the one that had swallowed him whole, without the gray lips and the gaping stormy mouth, but with the same intense, intelligent looking eyes. And the eyes were trained on Ted.

He felt a gentle wind touch his backside, coaxing him to move forward and he tentatively tested the first of the cloud-steps. It seemed to hold his weight though he still felt no surface beneath his foot. Ted climbed two more of the twelve steps of the cloud-staircase. Looking up, the face was gone and he quickly, but still very vigilantly, climbed the remaining steps.

Ted stood on the top step for a moment trying to make sense of what he was looking at. Colors, shapes, recognizable items obviously not formed by the cloud's movements and shades of blandness appeared before him in a small room with no walls, no ceiling, and seemingly no floor. It took a moment for his brain to register what lay before him.

It was a treasure room. But these were not the treasures of a king or a pirate. These were the treasures of a miser, a collector, someone who couldn't bear to part with anything once obtained. Or some sort of Lost and Found. There were books, articles of clothing, watches, eyeglasses, and suitcases. There were cardboard boxes and mail that looked ready for delivery, unopened. And a parachute.

Forgetting to be careful where he stepped, Ted moved quickly towards the parachute but noticed the gaping holes and ragged rips even before he reached it. He moved to the suitcases and began opening them, thinking he might find a sewing kit, could sew up the rips, repair the holes with some of the clothing that littered the small room, but found nothing that could manage the job. Inside one of the cardboard boxes he found some cheese and bread, but the cheese had long since turned to mold and the bread was too hard to break. Another box contained six bottles of wine and though he was not one that had ever enjoyed the drink, he did find a bottle opener and drained a third of one of the bottles in one tilt, if for no other reason than to prove to himself that he could taste it, that he was still alive.

Feeling a little woozy from the long gulp, Ted sat down on the floor that he could neither see nor feel and leaned against one of the larger suitcases. To his right were a black duffel bag and a tan briefcase, the final two items of the small treasure room that he hadn't yet opened. He pulled the briefcase to his side and looked at it, knowing that most businessmen didn't carry sewing kits in their attaché cases. He opened the case. He had never seen a bomb before, but he recognized the red cylinders and wires for what they were and quickly closed the case back up. On the top, just below the handle, he read the name Daniel Cooper engraved on a brass plate. Ted carefully put aside the briefcase and pulled the black duffel bag that had been next to it onto his lap and unzipped it. Money. Lots of money. Hundreds of hundred-dollar bills banded in bundles.

Maybe it was the wine. Maybe it was the realization of his position, where he was, what he was looking at, but Ted suddenly started laughing uncontrollably and couldn't stop laughing until his stomach hurt and his cheeks were streaked with tears. The cloud-face reappeared before him, the distance between them unclear, but the eyes seemed to be laughing right along with him. He decided he liked Mr. Cloud-Face. He thought they might even become friends.

*   *   *

Jim said good-bye to his teary-eyed mother and headed out to his car with his last suitcase. He had told her he could put off college for a year or two. He didn't want to leave her alone in the big house. But she insisted that this was his chance to expand his horizons, his turn to explore life and create a future for himself and she could never forgive herself if he put it off for her benefit and something ever happened to prevent him of this opportunity. She assured him that she would be fine, that she had lots of friends to keep her mind busy and time occupied. So he went.

It was a beautiful, late summer San Francisco day, a clear blue sky containing only a single large, white, puffy cloud. Jim had spent much of the last two years gazing into the sky. His father's body was the only one of the three that had never been found and he often wondered if it had returned to the earth at all. As Jim closed the hatch of his beat-up Omni, he glanced up at the solitary cloud and for a moment thought he saw a familiar face looking down at him, watching him. He smiled, tentatively gave the cloud a slight wave, and then, feeling a little foolish, quickly climbed into the car and headed for college.

The Ear

The Ear

Kelly walked the beach with her head down, scanning the sand for unbroken shells. It was early, the clouds hovering over the Atlantic, glowing orange and red as the sun began to peak out over the horizon, her favorite time of the day to be out shell shopping. An occasional jogger would glide by, nod with a smile or time a brief good morning between breath cycles as they pass. On the rare occasions that she had been out here later in the day during the summer, all she'd gotten were whistles from boys and young men that hadn't yet figured out that is the surest way to eliminate any chance of the fantasies inside their salacious minds becoming a reality. Even when she didn't hear the degrading cliché whistled in her direction, she felt their eyes on her, trying to dig beneath her clothes, as if there's anything there that isn't on every other human being of her gender. She always tried to ignore this type of attention, but it made her feel uncomfortable, like she'd been put on display. So the early mornings before going home to work with her finds had become her routine.

The mornings also provided her best finds. First crack at anything new that the tides brought in during the night, before they get trampled by children, sun worshipers, and wanna-be surfers. There were no real surfers on this side of the country. Once they actually got good enough to stand on their board for a short ride on a Carolina wave, they usually packed up and headed west for the other coast where the waves lasted longer than a handful of seconds and the curls occasionally broke above one's knees. But this was their training ground, for the attitude as well as the sport. They'd be running towards the water, surf board tucked under one arm, and stop in their tracks to watch Kelly walk by, undressing her with their eyes, oblivious to the look of disgust directed at them with her own eyes. So certainly during the summer months, Kelly stuck with the early mornings when the wanna-be surfers slept off the previous evening's beach activities and the vacationers were still gathering for an over-priced breakfast at Rosie's Cafe.

There was nothing new about New Lake, North Carolina. In fact, after living here for three years, Kelly was yet to even see a lake. But the town's stagnant growth had been part of the appeal to her when she had first arrived. This was a place that had chosen not to move on with the rest of the world. There were no McDonald's or Burger King or Denny's. And even though New Lake's continued existence depended on its annual draw of vacationers, there was no Ramada, Holiday Inn, or any other chain of any kind within the borders of the quaint, little town. The town's forefathers had long ago voted to keep out all brand name chains in order to sustain the feel of history and simplicity; however, several chains owned by some of the names just mentioned had opened for business a few miles outside the town's border, where the Freeway intersected the State Highway that led to New Lake. Every now and then, some brand name company like Blockbuster or Wal-Mart would come to town and try to petition a need for their particular expertise, but they never stayed long. New Lake was not going to change.

Rosie's was the only restaurant in New Lake that opened for breakfast. Most of the others were open by noon. There were four more restaurants in town, eight small motels with names like "The Sea Breeze", "Waterview", and "Motel." There were also three Bed and Breakfasts, and two gas stations with rickety old dispensers that still showed the gallons and price on a spinning wheel and didn't take credit cards at the pump. There was Missy's Hair Salon, Bob's Hardware where you could also rent beach supplies and surf boards by the day, and Crystal's Market where townies could still get credit if they came up a little short at the checkout. There was an eighteen-hole putt-putt golf course in bad need of repair, and an adjoining small race track lined with old tractor wheels to keep the kids and the go-carts on the pavement. The only theater in town had just one large screen and only showed second runs of films, shortly before they were released on video. All were locally owned and family run, some going on their fourth generation.

New Lake consisted of little more than 5000 year-round residents, but the population more than doubled from the beginning of June to the end of August with a constant onslaught of ever revolving vacationers. Money was tight in the off-season, but throughout the summer, everyone worked and usually made enough to get them from one season to the next. Kelly made things out of seashells and gave them to Rosie and Missy and several other local shops that were willing to put them on display in their stores and then sell them to admiring vacationers. It was purely a consignment deal, Kelly's take being 75%. Most of her creations sold for less than ten dollars, but she had to work very hard during the off-season to keep up with the summer demand of her trinkets.

Rosie had been encouraging Kelly to open up a little knick-knack shop of her own to sell them in, but Kelly didn't want the responsibilities and headaches and worries that usually accompanied ownership of a business. She didn't like the selling part, just the creating. Her creations sold like hot cakes during the towns prosperous months and every June she was ready with hundreds of little shell configurations that she had diligently put together for that purpose. She made tiny shell people and shell animals and shell furniture, carefully gluing tiny shells together to form their shapes and designs, mounting them on small blocks of driftwood. She made shell necklaces and bracelets and earrings. Her best seller was the simplest idea of all, shell bookends. Whenever she found a particularly large, heavier wrap-around shell (technically called a ficidae, but Kelly wasn't interested in what the different shells were called, just what they looked like and that they were intact) she would glue it to a varnished wood mount and voila, a book end. If she found two that were very similar in size and color, even better, a set of bookends. Vacationers bought her bookends as fast as she could find them and put them together. She didn't make a lot of money, but it put food on the table, paid the rent, and most importantly, it kept her busy.

It was the beginning of June and the vacationers had just started their annual invasion of the little ocean-side town. The seashells seem to be slim picking this morning and Kelly's mind wandered as she slowly scoped the area on the north side of the beach near a natural rocky border, an area where she usually found her best shells. The vacationers tended to stick to the southern side where it was all sand and water.

Kelly was alone in the world. She was an only child and her parents had been killed by a drunk driver on her nineteenth birthday. Two years later she had married. Her husband, a young New York City attorney fresh out of grad school with a very promising future, had been shot and killed when refusing to relinquish the keys to their new car to a mall parking lot mugger two weeks after they'd returned from their honeymoon. After the funeral, Kelly had taken the Greyhound south with no particular destination in mind, just a strong desire to forget and to start over. Somehow she had landed in New Lake. It was opposite everything she had experienced in her life in the city and felt it would be a good place to start a new life of solitude. She didn't own a car. She bought a bicycle for any treks too far to walk, but the town was small enough that her bike stayed locked up in the garage for the most part. Three blocks from the beach, she had rented out half a duplex from Rosie, who lived in the other half and had also become her best friend.

It had been Rosie that had given Kelly her first job as a waitress when she had decided to stay in New Lake. Waiting tables for the locals in the off-season hadn't been so bad, but once the vacationers started rolling in during her first summer in New Lake, she knew she wasn't cut out for the job. Rosie had agreed but was still willing to keep her on if she had wanted to stay, but Kelly only continued waiting tables long enough for Rosie to find a replacement. She had already started toying with seashells as a hobby to pass the time and occupy her mind, piecing them together into little figurines and stringing them into jewelry, and it had been Rosie's suggestion to display them for sale in a glass container by the cash register. Three years later, it was hard to walk into any place of business in New Lake and not find some of Kelly's creations displayed for sale somewhere within the shop.

She hated thinking about her past, what might have been, and Rosie was the only one she had ever told her depressing story to. She didn't want people feeling sorry for her, wasn't comfortable with their pity. To most who asked, though thankfully few ever did, she simply explained that she was from a big city and had desired a change of scenery.

Walking the beach usually helped her fight off the melancholy that occasionally tried to invade her thoughts. She found a larger, unbroken shell and put it to her ear, listening for the echoes of the ocean that had brought it ashore. A simple pleasure for a simple life. Feeling a little better with a good find, she carefully placed the shell in her tote back and continued her search. Another shell caught her eye and she picked it up, wiping away the caked wet sand. As she flipped it over in her hand, she immediately dropped it back into the sand as though it had burned her fingers.

At first she thought she had found a severed ear, but it felt no different than any other shell she had ever picked up as she had brushed away the sand. Regaining her composure, she stooped over the shell for a closer look without touching it. It looked like none she had seen before. She could tell that it wasn't actually a severed ear, but its resemblance to one was uncanny. Even the color had a fleshy pink tone to it. She flipped it over with her toe, still hesitant to pick it back up again. The smooth, rounded back side looked like any other seashell. She toed it over again in the sand. The hollow side had the same ridges as a human ear and swirled into a dark, small indention in its center. Tentatively, she picked the shell back up and, as she always did with each new find, put it to her ear to listen for ocean's soft echoes.

* * *

The sun was high in the sky when Kelly awoke. A boy, no more than seven, was standing a few feet away staring at her curiously.

"Jake! Get over here! Don't go bothering other people, now. Come back here right now!"

The boy turned to the voice of his mother who was lying on a blanket twenty yards south, a book resting open on her chest. "Her face is all red!" he exclaimed loudly, as he trotted back towards his mother.

"Well, that's why we use sunning lotion," she said as the boy approached. But the boy was just a few feet away from his mother by then, her voice had been discretely lowered, and Kelly briefly wondered how she had heard that reply from so far away.

Still shaking the cobwebs out of her mind, she tried to make sense of why she was waking up on the beach. She wasn't a sun worshipper. Her skin was fair and burned easily. She loved the beach and the ocean, but she never stayed out too long for fear of turning into a lobster. The sky was filled with large, white clouds shading the beach, the sun playing hide and seek behind them. A cool breeze came in off the ocean running its fingers through her long auburn hair. Looking at the placement of the sun, it had to be almost noon. She calculated that she had been asleep for more than three hours and had probably burned the side of her face that had been exposed. She glanced worriedly at her left shoulder that would have been equally exposed to the sun during her nap, and was surprised to see that it looked fine. A little extra color maybe, but didn't appear to have burned. She touched the left side of her cheek. No pain. No burn.

Brushing the sand from the right side of her face and out of her hair, off her right arm, and both her legs, Kelly stood up and tried to remember falling asleep on the beach, but she couldn't even remember lying down. She'd been looking for shells when…when what? It took a moment's pondering, and then she remembered. She'd found the weird looking ear-shaped shell. But that was all she could remember. Next was the boy standing over her, staring at her.

She looked around in the sand next to where she had been lying for the odd seashell, but didn't see it anywhere. She picked up the tote bag that carried her morning finds and dumped it out into the sand, thinking maybe she had dropped it in before she had fallen asleep. It wasn't there.

Shrugging it off, deciding it really didn't matter anyway, she piled her morning's take back into the tote back and trekked the three block walk home. Dropping the tote bag on the kitchen table where she did most of her work, she went to the refrigerator. She suddenly felt very hungry, as though her morning nap had drained most of her energy. Usually she skipped lunch, not because she was worried about keeping her trim figure, but merely because she wasn't a big eater. A light breakfast and a healthy dinner was her routine. But when she opened the refrigerator, she spied the hamburger she had been thawing for dinner and her mouth was practically watering for it. She pulled out the hamburger and placed it on the counter while turning on the stove. She grabbed a frying pan out of the cupboard and put it on the burner. She opened the package of hamburger and started molding the meat into a patty with her hands. The scent of the fresh meat made her mouth water even more. She raised the raw patty to her nose and closed her eyes as if beholding the fresh smell of a succulent rose for the first time. She took a large bite. Somewhere in her mind, she knew she should be disgusted by this, but instead she took another bite of the uncooked hamburger. She thought she'd never tasted anything better and before the stove had even warmed, she had devoured the entire patty as well as the rest of the raw meat from the one-pound package she had pulled out of the refrigerator.

She stood there in the kitchen for a moment, frozen as though in a trance, as her eyes shifted from the clean frying pan to the empty cardboard bowl that the hamburger had been packaged in. Had she really just eaten an entire pound of raw hamburger? Her mind refused to accept it as fact. She looked at her hands. They were sticky and smeared with remnants of raw hamburger and suddenly she felt sick to her stomach. She ran to the bathroom and saw her reflection in the mirror. Raw hamburger was smeared all over her lips and cheeks. The left side of her face was bright red as though it had been severely burned during her nap on the beach. Her brown eyes looked wild and wide mixed with panic and disgust. She leaned over the toilet, quickly opened the lid, and threw up before passing out on the floor.

Kelly dreamed that she was in a forest, hunting. She could smell her prey in the wind. It was not far now and she knew it could sense her presence. She could smell its fear. She was crouched in the tall weeds, silently closing in on the rabbit. Then she leaped and was on it, biting instinctively into its neck, sinking her long, sharp teeth into its squirming body as it put up a useless final fight. She drained the life from it and then she was flying. She had a bird's eye view of a field, a hawk's eye view of the gophers running in and out of their homes in the ground. Swooping down, she snagged a fat one, crushing it with her powerful talons before it even knew what had interrupted its day and she soared off into the sky again in search of an aerie to feast on her catch. She felt exhilarated, alive, invincible, and she heard herself roar. Now she was running full tilt on all four legs, chasing a family of deer. The youngest one stopped for the briefest moment to turn and look for its stalker, giving her just the extra second she needed to pounce on it, snapping its neck in one bite. The blood smelled fresh and tasted sweet. Then she was in the water, swimming through a school of small fish, her gaping mouth collecting all that was in her path.

A fly woke Kelly up. She was lying on the floor, still in the bathroom at the base of the toilet. She couldn't see the fly walking across her cheek and onto her lower lip, but she felt it. And she could hear it. Before she consciously knew what she was doing, she snapped her mouth open and the fly was trapped as quick as a frog snagging it with its long tongue. As she swallowed, another wave of nausea hit her and she got to her knees and leaned over the bowl as if she was going to throw up again, but nothing came up.

Confused, sore from lying on the hard tiled floor, she tried to pull herself together. If it hadn't been for the fly and the dried raw meat stuck to her lips and chin, she'd have tried to convince herself that it had all been part of the disgusting dream she'd had. She stripped off her clothes and climbed into the shower. The water felt too hot and she turned the knob to the left, unsatisfied until the knob wouldn't turn any farther and the water was icy cold.

Still unable to understand anything that was happening to her, she dried herself and got dressed. She needed to see a doctor. Lying out on the beach in the sun must have made her delusional. Looking into the mirror, she noticed her whole face was now a bright red and she decided she needed to see the doctor immediately.

She'd only been to Dr. Fendler's office once, shortly after arriving in New Lake. He had given her a prescription to help her sleep at night as she was still having difficulty at the time coping with the recent tragedies in her life. She hadn't told him of all that had happened, but merely that she was not getting any sleep. He operated out of his home, living upstairs and working downstairs. The nearest hospital was thirty miles away in Morehead City. He was a kindly old man, semi-retired, but all the townies went to him when not feeling well. She got onto her bicycle and headed towards his home office. A dog came bounding towards her barking as she biked past its home territory on the street. She turned the bike towards it, leaping off as she reached the grass and charged it. The dog, a small, twenty-pound, white beagle, shocked as much as she was by her sudden aggression, stopped wagging his tail and only had time for a whimper before she was on it, snapped its neck with her hands as her teeth sunk into it, all in a single fluid motion, just like she remembered doing in her dream.

It was like she was on auto-pilot. She knew what she was doing but could stop gnawing on the dead dog no easier than one could stop their own heart from beating at will. She was so disgusted she wanted to throw up again, but she continued to rip and tear at the dead dog's meaty throat, licking the blood from her lips between bites, savoring the taste of the bloody meat despite the disgust in her mind. She thought she was going insane. This couldn't possibly be happening. It had to be a dream, more realistic than any she had ever had before, but one she couldn't seem to wake up from.

A man appeared in the doorway of the house next door to the beagle's domain. He was yelling something at her as he began walking her direction. She dropped the dog at her feet, forgetting about her bicycle lying in the street and started running towards the beach. The wind blew back her hair. She felt something twitch on the left side of her face and instinctively brought a hand up to wipe away whatever was there. As she reached her left ear, she felt it move under her fingers. She touched it and realized she could only feel the touch with her fingers, her ear felt nothing at all. She pulled at the lobe and it retracted from her grip. If she didn't know that it was impossible, she would have sworn it had just shifted away from her grasp.

Just as she was about to accept the fact that she was truly going insane, she remembered the chain of events from the morning's walk on the beach. She remembered finding the ear-shaped seashell. She remembered putting it to her ear to listen for the ocean. And then she remembered passing out. She realized at once what had happened. Somehow that ear-shell had been more than a mere seashell. It had been a living entity. It had attached itself to her head, replacing her ear with itself, and had planted roots into her brain. She would have laughed at such a lunatic idea before today, but in her mind, she knew that was exactly what had happened. She had to get rid of it. She had to get the doctor to amputate the ear. It was the only way and she knew she was right.

Running down the beach, Dr. Fendler's beach-front home office only another two blocks ahead, she saw a young girl playing in the sand with her plastic shovel and bucket. Her course changed and she couldn't stop herself. She was running straight for the little girl; fresh blood, fresh meat, overwhelming her mind.

No! This isn't happening, she screamed at herself. She was going to attack this little girl and didn't think she had enough control over herself to stop. "Run! Get out of here! Go!" she started yelling at the girl as she charged.

The girl looked up from the bucket she had been busily filling with sand and smiled innocently, giving Kelly a shy wave. She didn't understand. Her five-year-old mind couldn't grasp the approaching threat for what it was. She wasn't going to move. Kelly was going to do to this little girl the same thing she had just done to the poor dog, snap her neck and have a taste of her flesh and blood. Running full tilt, Kelly purposely tripped up her feet sending herself flying face first into the sandy beach twenty feet before reaching the girl. By now the little girl was figuring out that this wasn't the way adults usually acted and she started to get up to run away. Kelly pushed herself back to her feet and continued her pursuit.

"Gloria!"

It was the mother. She had just noticed her daughter running towards her, away from a madwoman who appeared to be trying to chase her down. The mother began running towards her daughter.

One part of Kelly's mind thought that was fine, all the more blood to drink and all the more meat to eat. The girl was almost within her reach. Another couple of seconds and her need would be sated. The other part of Kelly's mind, the part that couldn't understand what the hell was happening, the part that was terrified beyond belief and seemed to be watching her own actions as though from a different body, did the only thing it could think of that had worked before, if only for a moment, and crossed up her running legs causing her to take another dive into the sand. As she pushed against the ground to get back to her feet, her left hand fell on a large stone in the sand and her fingers wrapped around it as she stood. As she started running at the child again, she brought the stone up and smashed it into the left side of her skull, aiming for her ear. She missed, or the ear dodged her attempt, and her own blood started running down her face from the gash in her head just above the ear. With one hand she reached out for the girl, just out of reach from her finger tips. Another step, maybe two and she'd be on her. The rock came smashing against the side of her head again, this time knocking her back to the sand. She pounded a third time, then a fourth, trying to kill the ear-shaped shell that had taken control and demanded the taste of fresh blood. She pounded once more with all of her might and the world went dark.

The little girl ran into her mother's arms, tears now streaking her terrified face. Her mother hugged her tight, burying her face in her shoulder so she couldn't watch the madwoman stoning herself to death with a rock. When the woman in the sand stopped moving, she backed away, slowly at first, then turned and ran as fast as she could towards town with her daughter, leaving her purse and blanket forgotten in the sand.

*   *   *

The event didn't make the news. The police hadn't believed the mother when she had told them that Kelly had been planning on murdering her child. Nor did they believe the old man when he told them Kelly had killed his neighbor's dog with her bare hands before starting to feast on her kill. That type of thing just didn't happen in New Lake and they certainly didn't need that kind of publicity if they were to survive the off-season. Her death was labeled a suicide brought on by severe depression once Rosie had informed Dr. Fendler and the sheriff of Kelly's recent tragic past.

Later that evening, just before the sun was dipping back out of sight for the night, a little boy was sitting next to his Dad on the beach, watching the waves roll in. He had a bucket full of collected shells sitting on his other side. He noticed a shell of a slightly different color, kind of a pretty pink, peaking out of the sand at his feet. He dug it out and rolled it around in his little hand.

"Look, Daddy," the boy said to his Dad. "This one looks like an ear!"

Not taking his eyes from the hypnotic motion of the evening waves, his father chuckled. "Well, you should certainly be able to hear the ocean good from inside that one then."

"Yeah, I bet you're right" the boy replied excitedly, as he brought the oddly shaped shell up to his own ear to give it a listen.

A Night at
Scruffy's Bar

A Night at Scruffy's Bar

My name is Dave. I am your average American nobody. I work to pay the bills and hope to have enough left over each week to have a little fun when not working. I am not into politics or saving the world as long as I can continue living my ordinary, routine life as comfortably as possible. Like most people, I live in my own little self-made world. I work about 35-40 hours per week every Wednesday morning through Friday morning, delivering a weekly community newspaper, paying my mortgage and bills five cents at a time delivering as many papers as I can deliver during the weekly delivery window. I will never get rich on this job, but I am very good at it after 35 years of practice and it affords me my home and enough to pursue my passion, playing pool.

I play pool in my off hours for fun. On Tuesday night, it's a 16-team league with my buddies at Cue Note, a pool hall with 13 nine-foot tables that are kept in great shape and the competition is generally pretty steep. On Friday nights, I run a little pool tournament at Scruffy's Bar, a hole in the wall sporting 3 seven-foot tables with beer stains on the felt and cigarette burns on the rails. The pool tables take up half the space in the bar making it not uncommon to be hip-checked by drunken beer drinkers squeezing through the narrow space between the pool tables and the seating tables to get to the restroom just when you were trying to sink the eight ball for a win.

Much like Cheers, Scruffy's has its regulars and everybody knows everybody's name. You are always greeted by someone calling out your name as a bell sounds when you walk in through the door and your beer is usually arriving at your table at the same time you do without the need to ask for it. The bartender on Friday nights, Nicole, is also amazingly good at seeing to it that you never have an empty beer sitting in front of you. I call it "the home of the magic beer." I will take a last swig from my bottle of Corona, turn to take a shot on the pool table, turn back to the seating table just a minute or two later, and my beer always seems to have magically refilled itself. Nicole will be already back behind the bar, filling a pitcher for others seated there. She smiles and nods when I tip the bottle her direction in thanks.

As I mentioned, I run a little double elimination 8-ball tournament every Friday night. Usually about 14-16 players join in. There is a $10 entry fee, and it pays out generally around $90 for first place, $50 for second place, and third place gets their entry fee back. We also give $10 to Nicole every week for opening up the coin operated tables for us so we don't have to put quarters in to get each game started. By the time the final game is played around 11pm each week, everyone has had their beers magically refilled by Nicole multiple times, rounds have been bought, shots have been passed around, and winning the tournament is less important than the comradery and laughter shared by the patrons.

The bar also features ten big screen TVs, five behind the bar and five more along the back wall behind the pool tables and up near the ceiling. Three TVs are always focused on sports, two more are on game shows, a couple will be showing whatever primetime dramas are playing on Friday nights, a couple will be featuring some form of reality TV, and one is always tuned in to CNN News. All ten with the sound turned off and subtitles turned on.

The conversation is light; laughter is always abundant and there is rarely an argument that Nicole can't douse quickly with a beer and a smile. It is a place where people come to forget about their lives outside the bar, their work, their financial stress, their personal struggles to get from week to week and year to year. The price of gas or the overbearing boss at work is put aside for a few carefree hours.

Tonight however, will be a different kind of night for everyone in the bar, a night they will always remember, a night where they will say, "I was there when it happened." Tonight, there is a little bonus for the winner of the pool tournament. First prize on the bracket board reads "$100 plus surprise mystery bonus!" Every single player in the tournament has asked me what that mystery bonus is, but I just tell them it will be revealed at the conclusion and the winner is named. Only Nicole and I know what the mystery bonus is and she has sworn to keep our secret even from the non-tournament regulars and customers at the bar until the time is right. I don't win the tournament every week, but I do win it about 30% of the time. A few of the regular tournament players that have won the first prize a few times in the past have told me tonight, "You're going down this time, Dave! I want that mystery bonus!"

But I *really* want to win tonight. I want the mystery bonus for myself, although to me, it is not a mystery. Tonight, I plan to focus on my shots, make the right decisions, and make it to the final game. Nicole will be replacing each beer with a water tonight, and then each water with another beer, to help me stay sure handed and focused on winning that final game when it comes around. I will certainly not be upset if I do not when the mystery bonus prize, assuming the winner wants it to begin with when they discover what it is, but I know what it is, and I want it, *passionately.*

Two of the ten TVs have been devoted to 24-hour news channels tonight and much of the conversation in the bar is on the subject they are covering. A few weeks ago, the president of Russia, Vladimir Putin, declared war on Ukraine. Putin has lied to the people of Russia to gain their support in his decision to invade the small country bordering Russia. He has lied to the world about his intentions and reasons for starting this war. While the rest of the world supports Ukraine and is trying to send them aid and resources to help them defend themselves against Putin's shameless attack, they are afraid to step in and put a stop to Putin for fear of starting World War III. Putin is unstable. He has been committing war crimes without conscience, targeting schools, hospitals, residential neighborhoods, without a single care or concern about innocent civilian casualties. The whole world knows Putin needs to be stopped immediately, but the whole world seems to be afraid to step in and actually stop him.

A few days ago, a Russian billionaire, Anatoly Fedorov, CEO of a software company, understanding that Putin is completely and totally out of control and on the brink of starting World War III, offered a million dollars to anyone who can arrest Vladimir Putin so he can be tried for his war crimes. His hope is that one of his close confidants, or one of his military high commanders, or a body guard or even Putin's wife, might come to realize the insanity he is instigating, the savagery and inhumaneness of his actions, and somehow turn him in to the UN, consequently saving thousands of innocent lives and possibly even preventing World War III…and then they could walk away with a million dollars to boot. No one knows for sure if Putin is the next modern-day Hitler, but do we really want to find out if he will go that far? Personally, I believe he has already gone far enough to fully justify ending his life in order save thousands of innocent lives. If someone had done the same for Hitler in his time, millions of innocent lives would have been saved. For all we know, the same could be true here. This is one time when we cannot afford hindsight. Foresight is necessary and must be acted upon. Putin must be stopped at any cost.

My girlfriend of the past eight or nine years, Tatyana, is Ukrainian and this has been a tough month for her. She has family back in Ukraine and has been sick with worry for their lives and her homeland, once beautiful, now ravaged and broken from Putin's senseless attacks. They, the Ukrainians, like us, like you and me, like your average Russian individual or family, like every single average nobody that make up the vast majority of the seven billion people on this planet, just want to live their lives comfortably. We just want to pay our bills on time, laugh with our loved ones and friends. We want to smile. We want to live our lives doing the things that we enjoy doing and we want the ability to wake up each morning without worrying that some greedy, insane politician somewhere out there is going to randomly bomb our neighborhoods and kill us or our family or our friends and change our lives forever just because they have some warped desire of power or control over the masses. People are people, we all basically want the same thing…to be happy. But a few of those people are monsters. Hitler was a monster. Stalin was another. Vladimir Putin is also one of those monsters.

And this was the topic of conversation with many at Scruffy's tonight. How do you stop Putin? When do you stop him? What risks are you willing to take to stop him? When is enough, enough?

Meanwhile, back in our own little world, we still had a tournament to play. The bar was packed and we had a full bracket of 16 players, all wanting to win that mystery bonus surprise. To make matters even more challenging, the men's restroom was locked shut with a sign reading "Massive Shit Inside – Out of Order" and everyone had to use the women's restroom which meant a constant line of anxious people needing to relieve themselves extending out near the pool tables. The people playing darts had to simply give up the game since the line to the restroom usually crossed through their line of fire to the dartboard.

In double elimination tournaments, one gets to lose twice before they are out of the competition. There is a winner's bracket and a 2nd chance bracket. The final game is the winner of the winner's bracket playing the winner of the 2nd chance bracket.

I won my first two games in the winner's bracket before Marco beat me, sending me to the 2nd chance bracket. Marco had won first place in the tournament last week but in the next game he played Kendra, playing with her snooker cue stick, who sent him to the 2nd chance bracket as well. I had to play Marco again in our loser's bracket and was able to win that time. Marco and I play a lot together and always seem to win as often as we lose against each other.

In the final game among the winners, Kendra, who had survived another round against Lee, was matched up against Charity, who also happened to be Nicole's mom. Despite the fact that Charity was Nicole's mom, Charity had been as equally unsuccessful at prying the secret of the mystery bonus prize out of Nicole as the rest of the bar had been.

Charity next sent Kendra to the 2nd chance bracket, I won my next match against Big Jim and the penultimate game was upon us. I had to beat Kendra to get to Charity, to get to the prize. It was a very close match, but Kendra missed a difficult 8-ball shot and I was able to run my final three balls and take the game. Now it was time for Charity.

Last time I had played Charity in the final match, she had won, so I figured odds were actually in my favor, but I needed to beat her twice, once to send her to the 2nd chance bracket with me, and then once again to win the tournament…and the prize. Nicole came over to replace my empty beer with a water and whispered in my ear, "That's my mom you are playing, you better win."

"No problem," I told her. "She won last time. It's my turn tonight."

"I hope so," Nicole said as she turned back to the bar.

Charity broke the rack and sank four balls before giving me a shot, but in the process, she had gotten rid of a lot of congestion on the table and freed up the only two of my balls that had been locked up together. I ran the table without giving her a chance to shoot again.

One down, one to go. Nicole looked a bit relieved.

My turn to break and I did pretty much the same as what Charity had done, knocking in five of my balls before missing. Charity then ran six of hers before missing.

Nicole was looking worried again.

I sank my last two balls but buried myself behind Charity's only remaining ball on the table and could not see the 8-ball cleanly. So, I decided to play it safe, I gently hit Charity's ball right up next to the 8-ball making it difficult to hit her ball directly into a pocket.

Nicole gave me a wink from behind the bar.

"My ball, off the 8-ball, off the rail, back here in the side," Charity said, and then added with a laugh, "as if that'll ever happen."

But then it did happen, exactly like she said, putting the 8-ball up against the top rail and the cue ball stopped in the dead center of the table.

Nicole gave me thumbs up.

Now I just needed Charity to miss a long bank and leave me a shot, any shot.

With most of the customers and players in the bar now watching intently with the night's championship on the line, Charity went for it. The 8-ball traveled the length of the table, center rail to corner on the opposite rail, but the ball rattled in the pocket and popped out, sitting right on the edge of the center of the pocket. The cue ball had slowly rolled all the way to the opposite side, opposite corner, and also rested on the edge of the center of the pocket. There was a collective "Ooooohhhhhh," in unison from the patrons as they waited to see which, if either, ball was going to make a slow, late drop into the pocket and ultimately decide the game one way or another. Neither ball dropped.

It was the longest possible shot on the table, corner to opposite corner and sitting on the edge of the pocket made it difficult to use any spins on the ball safely, but I have hit this shot a million times. All I needed to do was push the cue ball down the table at pocket speed, gently tap the 8-ball, and in it falls.

Piece of cake.

Maybe it was the adrenaline, not for the game itself, but for the prize that came afterward, that caused me to give it a little too hard of a push. The ball slowly traveled the length of the table, tapped the eight ball into the pocket, and then took another full two seconds to slowly follow it down the hole.

Cheers throughout the bar rang out for Charity. I like all the people that regularly show up at Scruffy's, the ones that always have a smile for you, always willing to tease you and then give you hug or a shoulder bump handshake, but they do love it when someone beats me in the tournament. Understandable. I win enough and I am always the first to congratulate anyone else that wins, and in truth, it wouldn't feel right if I won any more often than I do.

But I *really* wanted the win tonight.

After shaking Charity's hand and giving her a hug, congratulating her whole heartedly, and giving her four twenties and a couple of tens, I spotted Nicole behind the bar looking very distressed and staring at me, mouth shaped in a long "Noooooooooooo!"

"So," Charity said with a beaming smile, "I hate to win that way, but a win is a win. Now gimme my Surprise Mystery Bonus!"

* * *

We, the everyday normal Joes of the world, will all occasionally dream about what we might do if we had a million dollars. Retire, travel, pay off the credit cards and debts, by a house for mom, buy a boat, donate heavily to worthy causes…there are a million things one could do with a million dollars. And the Power Ball Lottery has actually made that dream come true for a few lucky people. Still, though I share in that common dream, I very rarely buy any lottery tickets. While the idea of winning millions and retiring early from my newspaper delivery business is quite appealing, the mathematical odds of my actually winning and the tightness of my monthly budget prevent me from justifying the forking over of a few bucks each week on such a long shot. I understand that you can't win if you don't play, but come on, 99.9% of the people that *do* play don't win either.

So last Sunday, when I heard about the billionaire Russian, Anatoly Fedorov, that wants to "contribute to the change of perception of Putin from an unquestionable ruler to somebody who is perceived by Russians as a criminal, and an illegitimate president who is essentially a usurper of power," as he put it in an interview with *Fortune magazine*, I had to stop and dream a little bit again about what I might do if I had a million dollars. But the idea of going to Russia, getting past his security, taking custody of Putin, or even shooting the slimy son of a bitch in the head, and then getting out again to enjoy my million-dollar bounty, was certainly even a longer shot than winning the lottery.

But still, we all dream, right?

I mean, let's think about it, really. Tala plays in the pool league on Tuesday nights. He's not on my team, but I know him pretty well and he has played in the Friday night tournaments once in a while. He is maybe in his late-forties or early-fifties, an Army vet, an ex-special forces guy, or so I have heard. Then there is Soloman, late-twenties, currently a math teacher, but was a pilot for the Air Force, now in the Reserves, shows up for the Friday night tourney whenever he can. There is Jordan, late-thirties, currently a commercial airline pilot that plays league and sometimes tournament. There's Dean, early-fifties, ex-Marine, a non-tourney regular at Scruffy's who collects guns and motorcycles. There are probably at least a dozen or more retired veterans in the 16-team league at Cue Notes.

Our own little private army? Yeah, right...dream on.

But what else have I got to do on a Sunday during the off-season of the NFL? So, I dreamed on.

I went to the Internet and spent about two hours finding out all I could about this Russian billionaire. Turns out Fedorov lives in California. It took me another 3 hours on the phone before I actually, unbelievably, finally connected with him.

"I have family in Russia that I am worried about," Mr. Fedorov explained. "Putin is jailing people that even LIKE a post that is against him. Can you imagine being jailed simply because you pushed a LIKE button for a post on Facebook? This is absurd! My family in Russia feels the same as I do about Putin. I fear they may be jailed just for believing as I do that Putin is a criminal."

"The million dollars you offer for his capture…" I began, but he cut in.

"Or his demise. Either way is fine with me. He simply must be stopped"

"I agree," I said. "And I would love to help. But I am lacking in resources and information. I am not a man-of-the-world, nor am I wealthy or experienced in this sort of thing. But I do have a Ukrainian girlfriend who is distraught for her family still in Ukraine. It pains me to see what she is going through and I would do anything I felt I could to help put a stop to Putin's tyrannical actions."

"Resources I cannot offer you. I offer the reward for his capture, but I must keep my hands clean of the activities," Fedorov said. "I cannot risk the safety of my family in Russia. Retaliation of my actions by loyalists must always be considered."

"I totally understand that," I told him. "How about information? I would assume you have contacts around the world, being who you are."

We talked for another hour…and then again three hours later for about ten minutes.

An idea was slowly evolving into a plan.

What I had learned was that Putin wasn't even in Russia at the moment. He was currently running his command out of India, specifically Berhampore, in the state of West Bengal. Fedorov had a contact that was fairly close to Putin, who also felt Putin had crossed the line between being human and being a monster, but was too frightened of him to take a stab at turning him in, even for a million dollars. But he was more than willing to let Fedorov know exactly where Putin was staying and the fact that he went on a guarded walk to the river each morning before monitoring the days attacks on Ukraine. He said Putin would only be there for another week before he was scheduled to return to Russia.

All this and a new contact number for Fedorov, in case I actually needed it, he relayed to me in our brief second phone conversation.

Then I made some other phone calls, starting with Tala and ending with one more brief call to Fedorov.

*   *   *

6am Wednesday morning, Tala, Soloman and Thad are getting themselves prepared on the east bank of the Hooghly River, about a mile south of Kumar High School on the southern tip of Berhampore, where Putin reportedly walks each morning with security for a little quiet time to think about his next ruthless move against Ukraine. Jordan is back in Manikganj, a small city on the western border of Bangladesh, staying close to the small plane that Fedorov had purchased under an assumed name Monday morning. All day Tuesday, Tala, Soloman and Thad had taken a small fishing boat north up the Padma River which borders Bangladesh and India. After getting just past Rajshahi, India, they had to travel ten miles through a forested area on foot, carrying their boat and supplies and all their fishing gear in case they had to prove that they were merely on a fishing expedition. That was the shortest stretch of land between the Padma River and the Hooghly River.

Once on the Hooghly, dressed in clothing to make them appear native to the area, they started traveling slowly south with the fishing gear in use, through Berhampore to its south side. They arrived just after dark Tuesday night and slept in the underbrush just off the shore, the boat completely covered and out of sight.

We didn't know how many bodyguards Putin took with him on his morning walk. Tala, who was given the command of this mission, was told to take no chances. If he felt they could not nab Putin without putting themselves in jeopardy, let it go. Fedorov was not concerned about any loses if we were unable to succeed. He was just very happy to see someone trying to earn his bounty. And since this whole affair had been my idea, I didn't want to be responsible for the deaths of any of my friends. This was not a suicide mission. This was a "let's just go see if we can pull it off" mission. If we fail, we fail. Come home with or without Putin, just make sure you come home.

6:15 Wednesday morning. Tala, Soloman and Thad are laying low in the bushes, rifles, supplied by Dean (and a day later reported as stolen) aimed at the path, silencers mounted, scopes in focus. Tala has told the other two that they will only fire shots if there was no doubt of success. They were not going to risk getting caught or killed.

"Shit," Thad said sarcastically. "We're here. We got this."

6:25 Wednesday morning. Putin is in sight, coming their direction, surrounded by six bodyguards, two in front, two in back, and one on each side of him, rifles very visible in their arms and at the ready.

"Why don't we just take them all out and be done with it?" Thad whispered.

"That would be nice," Tala replied, "and nothing less than the bastard deserves, but that is not what we are here for. If we can take him alive and get him back to the states to be tried for his crimes, that is what we do. But if he causes too much trouble and makes us shoot him before we get him back, that's up to him."

"You da boss," Thad whispered, never taking his eye from the sight.

"See that big tree at two o'clock?"

"Yes'" Soloman and Thad both whispered.

"Count two after they pass it and fire. Thad, you take the two in front. Solomon, the two in back. I got the last two." Tala instructed quietly. "All at the same time. No time for them to react. Head shots only. Quick kills. The second we see them all drop, we charge at Putin before he even realizes what's going on. First one there, zap him with your stun gun. Questions?"

Neither Soloman or Thad said a word.

The moment approached, the Russians passed the tree, "whooomp, whooomp, whooomp" sounded almost simultaneously as the men surrounding Putin dropped to the ground, and Putin stood there looking at them trying to figure out if he had also been hit or not. Two seconds later, he turned our direction just in time to see Soloman hit him in the chest with a stun gun and Putin fell as well.

Suddenly Soloman whipped his body sideways as blood spurted into the air. Tala, already facing that direction looking for any witnesses to their assault saw the remaining bodyguard that had stayed back watching Putin's six taking aim for another shot. But Tala got off the shot first and the bodyguard fell to the ground firing his second shot into the sky as he dropped.

Soloman had only been hit in the arm and the bullet had pierced a muscle and exited out the other side. Thad quickly tied a tourniquet to Soloman's arm to stop the bleeding and the two of them joined Tala as they pulled the bodies out of view into the brush.

Soloman and Thad covered them up to be found later when people came looking for them. Tala dragged Putin over to the fishing boat, got the boat quickly back into the water, got Putin into the boat, tied his hands to his feet, and covered him with a tarp. Then all the fishing gear was laid out on top of the tarp.

Unlike the trip down, they used the motor of the small fishing boat on the way back up the Hooghly River. The toughest part was going to be the ten-mile trek through untamed forest to get back to the Padma River. It was hard enough carrying the boat and equipment through their first time; this time they had Putin's dead weight to carry as well.

They ditched all the supplies except the rifles, hiding them under leaves and behind bushes. With the rifles slung over their shoulders, they left Putin in the boat and the three of them lifted it and half jogged the ten miles in just under two hours' time. Soloman's arm hurt like a bitch, but the adrenaline running through his veins as they carried a cancer of the world on their backs allowed him not to give the pain much thought.

Exhausted, sore, and gasping for breath, they dropped the boat into the waters of the Padma and gave Putin another zap from the stun gun, not so much to keep him knocked out, but rather to make him hurt a little more for the way they all felt after that ten-mile jog.

At 5pm, they abandoned the boat and loaded themselves and Putin into the jeep they had used to get from plane to boat on Tuesday morning.

By 5:30pm, Jordan had lifted off and they were on their way home.

*   *   *

Nicole came over and stood in front of the men's restroom with the key in hand. I led Charity over to the door as well, and about 12 people followed us even though no more than four or five could fit in the short narrow hallway leading to the restrooms.

"The prize is in there?" she asked. "Is that why it's out of order?"

"Here's the deal, Charity," I explained. "You can take what's behind door number one here and get an opportunity to earn a million dollars, or you can take one hundred thousand dollars cash right now that I have in the back of my car in the parking lot."

Nicole was looking at her mom, shaking her head, pointing to the parking lot.

"Do I get to see what's behind the door before I decide?" Charity excitedly asked. She was practically jumping up and down where she stood though her feet were not leaving the ground.

"Sure, why not. You should be able to make an informed decision. Go ahead," I said, turning to Nicole. "Open her up."

Nicole removed the "Massive Shit Inside – Out of Order" sign and put the key in the lock. She took one more pleading look at her mom and then swung the door open.

The bar became silent. The dozen or so crowded around the door had their jaws open and stared in shock and disbelief. The rest of the patrons in the bar sensed from the quiet, open-mouthed stares as the door came open that something was amiss and the quiet became instantly contagious.

Sitting on the closed toilet seat, leaning forward with each hand handcuffed to its respective ankle and a red ball-gag held in his mouth and tied tightly around his head, eyes wide and scared to death, sat Vladimir Putin. In the opposite corner of the small bathroom, next to the empty pizza box and six empty bottles of Corona, stood Tala, gun in hand, pointed at Putin's head. Aislynn, another bartender at Scruffy's who wasn't working this night, had supplied the ball-gag and the handcuffs. She didn't ask me what I needed them for, and I didn't question why she happened to own two sets of genuine police handcuffs

"You are the winner tonight, Charity," I told her. "If you want to pull the trigger, you get a million dollars, but you will also need to take on a new identity and leave your family and friends behind. It would all be arranged for you in the next couple of hours. Or you can take the hundred thousand as your first-place prize and go on with your life unchanged, just a bit richer."

"Mom," Nicole pleaded. "Take the hundred grand. Let someone else be the hero."

"No worries, Nicole. As much as I would love to shoot this asshole in the face, I don't want to leave you and Brittney," Charity said. "I give the honors to the next in line in the tournament."

"I was hoping you would," I told her. "I had, in fact, already planned on it."

I nodded to Tala, he handed me the gun, and without a second's hesitation, I ended Vladimir Putin right then and there.

*　　*　　*

After the gun went off in the small bar, no one was able to speak. It had happened quickly enough that most of the patrons in the bar still had no idea what was going on. All they could see was a bunch of people with silenced shock on their faces and me aiming a gun into the bathroom and pulling the trigger.

No one ran for the door. No one screamed in fear. They all know me. They know I am not a threat to anyone in the bar. And of course, they still wanted to know what the hell that surprise mystery bonus had been.

Less than two minutes after the shot was fired, three men swooped in and carried Putin's corpse out of the bar and loaded him into the back of a black SUV. Two more carrying a suitcase came in right after them and went into the bathroom closing the door behind them. A few people around the bar were starting to whisper, but most were still trying to figure out what had just happened and, still in shock from tonight's events, couldn't find the words to speak even if they had wanted to.

Five minutes later, the bathroom door opened and the two men left. The bathroom was spotless and ready for use again.

I signaled to Nicole to keep everyone quiet and here and I walked out the door behind the two men, as we had previously planned that I would. I returned a moment later with two suitcases of my own, one in each hand, and joined Nicole behind the bar. All eyes were on me. No one was speaking a word.

"First of all," I said, "I want to thank you all for being my friends. I am happy to have gotten to know most of you and I hope you will forgive me for my actions tonight, but it was something I felt had to be done. The body carried out of here tonight, the person who I just killed with no trial and a point-blank shot to the head, was Vladimir Putin."

A collective gasp and whispering immediately started among the 45 patrons in the bar.

I raised my hand signaling that I had more to say and they quieted down.

"Putin has been missing since Tuesday, but the Russians are keeping it quiet, probably waiting to find out if he is dead or being held for ransom or being put on trial. They will not be able to keep it quiet after tonight. The men that came in and got him will be making his death public and proof-positive tomorrow morning. This, we are hoping, will put an end to the war on Ukraine and eliminate any possibility of the start of World War III."

I paused to take a sip from the Corona that had magically appeared next to me on the bar.

"I realize that what I did may not have been the proper thing to do, but it was what I believed to have been the *right* thing to do. With the help of some of my friends who will remain unnamed at this time, we were able to capture Putin with the intent of turning him in to be tried for his war crimes. When we got him here, when he was delivered to me, I looked into his eyes and I clearly saw the monster inside and instantly knew that I would not be turning him in. I couldn't take the chance that he would somehow be allowed to walk free. Again, right or wrong, I can't say. But it was something I felt needed to be done.

"As a result, I will be getting unofficially relocated with some unofficial help from some people that agree with what I chose to do. They first tried to get me to tell them where Putin was being kept yesterday, unofficially, but didn't try too hard and decided to look the other way when I told them what I had next planned to do with him.

"In this first suitcase here," I continued, laying the first one on the bar and pushing it towards Charity, "is Charity's Surprise Mystery Bonus of one hundred thousand dollars for winning the pool tournament tonight. In this second case is one hundred thousand more to be divided up evenly among the rest of you just because you are here, because you are my friends, and because you listened to me say my piece and explain my actions.

"I will not ask you to not talk about tonight or to not post what happened here on Facebook or Twitter or what-have-you. But I will ask you to wait until after 12 noon tomorrow before you do so. By then, the men that left here tonight with his body will have created their own story and provided pictures to the media as proof of his death and whatever you say, and to whomever you say it, will probably not be believed anyway. I mean, come on, with an official story about, and proof of, his death all over the news worldwide, who's going to believe you when you say you say Putin assassinated in the men's room at Scruffy's Bar last night.

"Thank you all very much. Nicole will now split up the cash and hand it out. Please, no one leave the bar until everyone has received their mystery bonus surprise tonight. And once again, it's been nice knowing you all. Take care. I'm outta here."

I am writing this narration of that night at Scruffy's Bar under an assumed name. Not even my publisher knows my real identity or where I am currently living. Anatoly Fedorov had indeed been very generous with his money. Tala, Soloman, Thad, and Jordan also each received a million dollars from him for their part in the capture of the monster, as did I for getting it all put together and ultimately putting an end to Putin's reign of terror. And Jordan was even told he could keep the plane.

When the news and pictures of Putin's demise came out the next day, the war on Ukraine did indeed cease immediately and the successor to Putin even pledged to help Ukraine rebuild what Putin had just destroyed.

It was out of my million that I gave two hundred thousand to the patrons of Scruffy's. I figured Tatyana and I would do just as fine starting our lives over someplace new with new identities and the remaining eight hundred thousand.

Piece of cake.

About the Author

David Brooks lives in Palm Coast, Florida, where he is retired after 36 years in the newspaper business. He spends his time playing competitive pool, reading his favorite authors, and writing stories. *It's Only a Dream* is his fourth book, following *The Master Plan, As Fate Would Have It*, and *JuCLuCee*. Currently David is working on his fifth book, due out in 2026, called *Beyond the Call of Duty*.

David can be contacted at david@horizonroad.com.